MY OUT OF TOWN BAE

TOSHA LAVETTE

My Out Of Town Bae

Mailing List

To stay up to date on new releases, plus get information on contests, sneak peeks, and more,

Go To The Website Below...

www.colehartsignature.com

CHAPTER ONE

TAY

"Dontavious, where the hell do you think you're going?" Nina asked as she caught me trying to ease out of bed. If it were up to her, she would have continued to watch me sleep instead of waking me up.

"Nina, roll your thick ass over and go back to sleep. You already know where I'm going. I'm going home. Why the fuck did you let me fall asleep over here, anyway? You know I don't even do no shit like this. I can't keep doing this shit."

"You were sleeping so peacefully that I didn't want to disturb you. What's the big damn deal anyway, Dontavious?"

"You stay on bullshit, Nina. That's why I don't fuck with you like I used to. Now I have to go home and listen to Amor's bullshit."

"You wouldn't have to listen to her bullshit at all if you'd just be with me," Nina whined as she looked up at me with those big, pretty eyes.

I hated it with a passion when she started to act like that. We'd been doing the shit forever, and she still couldn't seem to get with the program.

"Nina, you know damn well that shit will never happen. I see you like to hurt your own feelings, don't you? How many ways can I tell you the same shit?" I vented.

"I don't, Dontavious. I hate that shit, to be honest. But while your big-headed ass is trying to be funny, riddle me this. If you love that bitch so much, why the hell are you fucking me? What, her pussy ain't good or something?" Nina quizzed.

"Your pussy ain't fuckin' with Amor's, so don't get beside yourself. Watch your fuckin' mouth, too. Don't ever call her out of her name again," I snapped.

Nina knew I didn't play that shit. When it came down to Amor, she knew to stand down.

"Whatever, nigga. Get your shit and get the fuck out, then. Since that's how you feel. Nobody's forcing you to be here. You're here because you choose to be. I'm not holding a fucking gun to your head," Nina rambled.

The only problem I had with her ass was that she didn't know when to shut the fuck up. Like the Energizer bunny, her mouth kept going and going.

"I was about to do that anyway, with your goofy ass. I'll be back over here later, though. Keep that thang tight for daddy. Please don't have that same fucked up ass attitude when I get back."

"Nigga, fuck you. You don't even have to come back. Stay at home where your b—I mean your girl is since that's the one you love so much."

"Yeah, that's what the fuck I thought. I was waiting on you to correct that shit," I responded with a slight smirk on my face.

When I got in my whip, I peeped the time again, and it was a little after two in the morning. I was already in hot water and had the nerve to still be fucking up. I thought about what kind of excuse I could give Amor for why I was out so late again.

That was the second time I'd pulled the same stunt, once with Nina and once with another chick I was smashing from around the way. I'd promised her that I wouldn't do the shit again, and I honestly had no intention of letting her down. I had the worst luck when it came to dealing with females, Nina's ass especially. She always had some slick shit up her sleeves. I knew I wouldn't be able to deal with her ass for too much longer.

Nina was a dope ass female, but she required way too much from me. The things she required, we both knew I couldn't be the nigga to give it to her. I couldn't even stunt like she wasn't deserving of those things, but her thinking I would leave Amor for her was where shit started to crumble between the two of us. That shit wasn't about to happen. How she even got that idea, I didn't know, but she was barking up the wrong damn tree.

For years, I'd been navigating through life, trying to keep them both happy. If Nina was happy and getting her way, I didn't have to worry about her getting in her feelings and getting on that drama and messy shit. But the first time I did or said something that wasn't appeasing to her, all hell broke loose. I was tired of letting her back me into a fuckin' corner. Hell, my own woman didn't try me on that level, so a bitch I was just fuckin' wouldn't be allowed to do the shit either. There were levels to that shit.

Every time I'd attempted to break things off with her, she found a way to make the shit not happen. It was simple with Amor. As long as I wasn't doing shit to embarrass her or make her look like a fool, she was cool. I could only respect that, and I tried my best to keep my end of the bargain. All I had to do was keep some money in her pockets, feed and fuck her good, and she was happy. Amor wasn't hard to please. She'd never been, and I loved that about her.

I couldn't even stunt. I fucked with Nina and her son, Jay,

the long way. That was my lil' nigga, and he could get anything he wanted and needed from me, and she knew it. I knew how much he looked up to me, which was part of the reason I decided to stick around, even when his mama worked my damn nerves. I liked being a father figure in his life. That shit made me feel like I was doing something right for a change. The feeling was rewarding and something I really couldn't explain. I was a coldhearted nigga, though. Let these bitches tell it.

I called my nigga Derrick to let him know the lie I was about to tell Amor when I got to the crib. He would be the first person she contacted to see if I was really where I said I was. It was a Saturday night, and Derrick and I were known for hitting the clubs occasionally on the weekends. It was the only logical lie I could think of. He hated when I put him in those awkward situations because he liked Amor and hated when I mistreated her.

Derrick always stressed the importance of having a good woman. Of all the niggas in our crew, he was the only one who wasn't on bullshit. He didn't have an ole lady, but whenever he did decide to take a female seriously, that nigga was all about her. He didn't do the cheating shit whatsoever. I looked up to him and respected him for that and reasons beyond.

Everyone in my circle knew I had a good woman by my side, and they didn't understand why I did half the shit I did. Normally, a man cheated when he wasn't happy or satisfied at home. With Amor, neither of those were factors because she held shit all the way down. I realized I was just a selfish ass nigga. I didn't deserve Amor or all that she'd been to me, but I was thankful she stuck beside me when she could have chosen to walk away on several occasions. I knew without a doubt that she loved a nigga to death. That and her loyalty to me spoke volumes.

When it came to our relationship, I was the problem. I didn't have a single complaint about Amor. For the longest, she had been the closest thing to perfection. That woman deserved the world, and I struggled with the fact that I couldn't give it to her. I didn't know why the shit was so complicated when loving one woman should have come naturally to me.

I went back and forth with myself all the time and wondered why I couldn't be the man she needed or wanted me to be. I didn't even know why I needed two or three extra bitches to validate me when neither of them could compare to what I already had. Keeping my tool in my pants had become the hardest thing for me to do. With the way bitches threw themselves at me, I couldn't even see it changing. I knew I needed to work on myself because Amor was tired of dealing with my bullshit. Lately, she had been expressing it more than ever.

Amor walking away wasn't even an option for me. As far as I was concerned, I'd welcomed her to Death Row. The only way out of this shit would be if one of us were to die. She was mine, and no matter what I had going on, I couldn't see myself doing life without her. Another nigga would never be able to get his hands on her if I had anything to do with it. Amor knew not to even put a nigga in danger like that.

When I got home, I took a quick shower in the downstairs bathroom. I didn't want to risk waking Amor up and having to answer the many questions she would have about why I came in and got straight in the shower. I could smell Nina's perfume all over me, and if I could smell that shit, I knew my girl would too. That was an argument I didn't even have time for.

When I made it to our bedroom, Amor was fast asleep. There was a half-empty bottle of wine on her nightstand beside the bed, so I knew she was out of it. I gently eased into bed and tried to drift off to sleep. I was so glad I didn't have to go back and forth with her, at least not until she woke up with some shit she needed to get off her chest, as she always did.

CHAPTER TWO

AMOR

I sat up on my side of the bed, watching my boyfriend Tay's phone constantly vibrate. Normally, the motherfucker would be so far out of dodge that I wouldn't have even been able to see it. I guess he was so tired when he crept into the house after two in the morning that he'd forgotten to hide the motherfucker. So far, it had gone off four times. I knew it had to be one of his hoes blowing up his shit because what would a nigga have wanted at that time?

Those side bitches of his were really getting out of line, and they just didn't give a damn anymore. I'd been letting so much shit slide, but I was at the point where I was ready to go upside his head and theirs. Although I tried to let the crazy side of me rest, this nigga was about to bring that bitch out of retirement. I was so tired of being a crazy bitch, when all I wanted was some peace in my life. I wanted to be soft and feminine, but dealing with a nigga like Tay, that shit wasn't even possible.

The disrespect was at an all-time high. As a woman, I couldn't even see myself blowing up the phone of another bitch's man in the wee hours of the morning. I was a different breed, though, and the shit I encountered with other bitches proved that to me damn near daily. The self-respect these bitches lacked was sickening. I could never go out so sad about a nigga who didn't have me up. Shit was sad out there and only got sadder by the day.

One thing was for damn sure—Tay was slipping when it came to keeping his hoes in line. I wasn't dumb enough to believe he would stop entertaining other women, and I wouldn't have dared waste my time to ask him to. All I asked was that he keep the shit away from me. I didn't want to hear shit about a bitch, and I damn sure didn't want to hear shit from a bitch. When a bitch felt like she was bold enough to approach me about my nigga, it became a problem. That meant he was making these bitches feel way too comfortable. Other than that, I was cool until my peace was fucked with.

I was aware of everything, but I wasn't bothered by shit until it started to touch my front door. Over the years, I'd done some growing and wouldn't even approach a bitch about my man unless I was provoked. Besides, I wasn't the one with any points to prove. That nigga belonged to me until I said otherwise. The problem was, the other bitches knew that, and it drove their asses crazy. I wouldn't dare give a bitch the satisfaction of feeling like I was bothered. They were coming for me, which meant I had to be doing something right. I couldn't stand a 'want to be relevant' ass bitch. Those bitches were as messy as they came.

Tay often used that being a street nigga shit as an excuse to get out of the bullshit that always tended to pop up. The vibration of his phone was loud as hell, so I knew he heard the shit just like I heard it. Of course, I wasn't blind to all the bullshit niggas encountered in the streets, and I knew that shit could happen at any given time. But I knew my nigga like the back of my hand. I was so sure it was a bitch on the other side of that phone that I was willing to put it on his head. No longer could I be fooled by anything he had to say. I knew what it was, and for the life of me, I couldn't understand why he always tried to pull the wool over my eyes.

The goofy ass nigga didn't even flinch. He continued to lay there and fake snore like he didn't have a care in the world, which only irritated me further. I wanted to punch him dead in his shit, and I probably would have gone through with it if I thought I could have gotten away with it. Sometimes I really didn't know what kind of fuckin' fool the nigga played me for. Fed up wasn't the word for what I was. The more chances I gave his ass, the more he tried to play in my face.

My leaving was the only thing that would wake his dumb ass up, and that was right around the corner. I could damn near feel myself about to walk out of his life. One thing I knew for sure was that he would never see it coming. Tay thought I would forever be stuck on stupid, but my dumb bitch days were about to end.

I'd always known I deserved better, but for some reason, I stuck around as women often did, praying that the man I loved would change for me. The realization that he would never get right fucked with my mental and broke me down emotionally, but there was nothing I could do about it. If there was one thing I'd learned, it was that a man was gon' be a man for sure. It didn't matter how good of a woman they had waiting for them at home. Pussy could make men do the dumbest shit. It was like power to some men, though, and they would risk everything they had for a new piece of ass.

"Nigga, who the fuck is steadily calling your phone at this time of the morning? And don't lie," I asked, tapping Tay on the shoulder to wake him up.

"Amor, don't start with that bullshit. That's probably just

one of my niggas. You already know what's going on with me," he nonchalantly responded.

"Why the hell would one of your niggas be calling your phone restricted, Tay? Please quit playing in my face like I'm one of those dense hoes you're used to fuckin' with," I snapped.

"Damn, Amor, you act like I can call the number back to see who it is. Take your black ass back to sleep. Or better yet, since you're up, go fix a nigga some breakfast or something. Always trying to start some shit over nothing," he said and mumbled some other shit that he knew better than to say out loud.

"Nigga, fuck you. Get whatever bitch that is calling you to fix your black ass some breakfast. I'm sick and tired of you and the games you play. Just keep that same energy when I pull a you on you."

"What the fuck did you just say to me, girl?" Tay snapped.

I could hear the anger in his tone, but I didn't give two fucks. He wanted to play, so I was about to play with his ass. I knew exactly what to say to get under his skin. Hell, half the time, I wished I meant the shit I said to him. If I was a dirty bitch, I would have been walked that nigga like the dog he was. But, no, I just had to be one of the good ones.

"Nigga, you heard what the hell I said. It's cool when you do it, so don't let it be a problem when I start doing it."

"Amor, quit playing with me like I won't beat your ass. Find you a toy or something for real. This ain't even that."

"You know damn well you ain't gon' put your hands on me, nigga. My brothers would fuck you up so bad but carry on."

"I'm not worried about your weak ass brothers, Amor. Those niggas know who to play with." There was so much cap in that nigga's rap because he knew they would get on his ass about me.

I'd been dealing with Tay's shit for the past six years. I met him when I was sixteen, and he was clocking twenty. I was young and naïve, knowing nothing about the natural world or how cold it could be. As most niggas would have done, Tay used that shit to his advantage. He saw me as fresh meat that had never been tampered with. I met him at a party I wasn't supposed to be at, but my friend Leilani talked me into going anyway. Dealing with Leilani, I stayed in some bullshit and often got in trouble with my parents. But, if she was down for it, I was down for it too. There were never any questions asked either.

Don't get me wrong, I may have been a little rebellious at times, but my head was on straight. I enjoyed turning up as much as the next female did, but I wasn't on any hoe shit. I was a virgin and planned to keep it that way. At least until Tay came into the picture, and my gullible ass fell for his charming ways. From the beginning, I was weak in the knees for that nigga, and all these years later, I still couldn't stand the fuck up. The shit was pathetic, and I knew it.

Tay acted as if he'd never met a girl who was still a virgin, which said a lot about the girls in my hood. I was his and his only; that was one of his biggest flexes. Not to mention, I was as pretty as they came with a body like the bitches on the cover of a magazine. My beautiful chocolate skin was flawless, I had full, juicy lips, and my natural hair reached my lower back.

When we met, Tay let me know I was different, unlike any other chick he'd ever been with. I never really understood what he meant, but I always took it as a compliment. Besides, I'd seen some of the bust-downs he had been with and wasn't the least bit impressed. I joked about his lack of taste in women all the time. I was his trophy, and we complimented each other perfectly.

Tay was what most would call *that* nigga. You know, the nigga all the bitches flocked to. The one every female in the hood wanted a piece of. When bitches looked at him, they saw a come up because he came from a family with money, and they wanted a piece of it. Not only that, but he did his illegal activities on the side. Money was never an issue with him.

So, of course, I was honored to be the chick on his arm. I wasn't the type of female who was moved by material things, so what he had in his pockets never mattered to me. I was with him because I wanted to be with him—not for anything he did for me, even though he did a helluva lot.

Being Dontavious's girl came with more drama than I could have ever imagined, from beating a different bitch's ass every other day to getting kicked out of my parent's house as a result of my rebellious ways. I was the true definition of a good girl gone bad. Often, I wished I had taken my mother's advice and stayed my ass in a child's place.

The vibration of Tay's phone once again snapped me out of the daze I had been in for the longest. Obviously, whoever was calling wanted some attention, and I decided it was only right that I gave them just that. I was in the mood for straight bullshit at that moment.

I knew the nigga wasn't sleeping, and he acted like he didn't hear the shit, so I grabbed the phone, went into the other room, and answered it. I figured it had to be important since whoever the bitch was decided to keep calling us. His phone wasn't an iPhone; that motherfucker was an our-phone.

"Hello?" I greeted.

"Who the fuck is this? And why are you answering my man's phone?" a female voice asked.

"Your man? I think there's been some kind of mistake because you can't possibly be talking about the nigga whose beard still has my coochie juices in it."

"Ummm, can you put Dontavious on the phone, please?"

"Bitch, Dontavious is sleeping, and I'm about to join him.

Stop calling us and find something safe to do. I'm warning you, this ain't it!" I snapped.

"Amor, you're really doing too much. I'm sure he wouldn't appreciate you answering his phone. Now, would he?"

"I'm glad you know who the fuck I am. I want you to be just as aware when I catch your ass."

"Wait a minute, bitch. Let me tell you somethi—"

Click!

I hung up the phone before she could say whatever she felt she needed to tell me. Had she called straight through, I would have had more respect for the bitch, but those no Caller ID games were for kids. I didn't have time for it, and I wasn't about to play the radio with no bitch about a nigga who came home to me every night. I knew Tay wasn't shit, and he probably never would be, but he was mine, and I chose to stick beside him. The way I looked at it, there was no bitch alive who could bully me out of that man's life.

I wasn't leaving him until I was good and ready. I ran shit when it came to his no-good ass. That wasn't a flex, but a bitch had me messed up, thinking she could handle me any kind of way. I was the one who did the handling. The bitch referring to me by name let me know she knew the nigga she was fucking was in a relationship with someone else. So, she really didn't have any excuse. She was just as trifling as he was. Whoever the bitch was, she did right to play *69 games. I dared the bitch to hang up and call straight through. All I needed was her phone number to find out all her personal information. I hated to be on crazy shit like that, but it was whatever once I felt disrespected. Whoever that hoe was, she tried it.

As long as my bills cleared every month, I had everything my little heart desired, and no bitch ever felt the need to approach me in person about *my man*, I was good. Tay could have all the little fun he wanted because when it was my turn, that nigga was going to need Jesus and all his disciples. After dealing with the same shit for so long, I couldn't even find the strength to argue with his ass, but I couldn't let it slide either. I had to speak on it, or it would bother me forever.

When I walked back into the bedroom, Tay was suddenly awake and looking around for what I assumed was his phone. Before I knew it, I had tossed that motherfucker at his face, hitting his ass right in his mouth. I smiled when I saw blood start to drip. That was exactly what his ass got for trying to be sneaky. I wanted to pop his ass again, but it wasn't even worth it. Some shit would never change.

"Oww, Amor! What the fuck is wrong with your stupid ass?" Tay angrily asked.

"I'm sick of your lying, cheating ass, that's what. That unknown number called your ass again, and I answered. All I know is if you're somebody else's man, you need to take your ass wherever this bitch lives, so she can deal with your bullshit. Got this bitch asking me why I'm answering her man's phone and demanding me to put you on the phone," I verbalized.

"I don't know what you're talking about, man. That's probably just somebody playing on my phone, and you're falling for it. I told you about getting all worked up over nothing, baby," he lied again.

"Tay, please, or Dontavious, as she called you. Like I said, it's all good. I don't even know why I'm wasting my breath because yo' ass is never going to change. The crazy part about it is, I know that shit," I expressed, on the verge of tears. But I wouldn't dare give that nigga the satisfaction of seeing a tear fall from my eyes.

"See, now yo' ass is tripping for real. Move around with all that!"

"Yeah, I'm about to move around, aight. I'm going to get

my hair and nails done. After that, I'm going shopping, all on you," I informed, daring him to disagree.

"Shiiid, that's nothing new. You do that shit all the time anyway," Tay retorted.

"Yeah, that's true, but I'ma swipe everything but your name off that card today, and I dare you to say anything about it when I get back."

"Whatever, Amor. Do what you do. I'm not tryna go back and forth with you all day."

"That's what I thought you'd say."

"I'm serious, baby. I don't know who that was on the phone, but I'm sorry it upset you," Tay lied again.

"Tay, go to hell!" I exclaimed.

Before I started getting ready to leave the house, I shot my best friend, Leilani, a text and asked if she wanted to have a girl's day out. She immediately texted back to let me know she was down. Leilani just didn't know it, but it was her lucky day because she would get a free ticket today, and there was no limit to what she could throw in the bag. Tay had me fucked up, and I planned to hit his pockets all the way up. It wasn't like he would miss the shit, but it still made me feel like I was doing something.

It was a damn shame that I wasn't even mad to find out that he was back on his bullshit. Was I hurt? Maybe a little, but it was nothing that I wouldn't soon get over. Tay was full of words with no actions. To me, the best apology was changed behavior, and I wasn't getting any of that from him. Therefore, when he apologized, the shit went in one ear and right out the other one. I'd heard all the shit before, and as far as I was concerned, this time wasn't any different. The good thing about being burned so many times was that each time hurt less than the previous time. I was somewhat numb to all of it. I couldn't trust the nigga as far as I could throw him.

Once I was dressed, I stood in front of the gigantic mirror in our bedroom and admired myself. I didn't toot my own horn enough, but I was straight pressure, even though my nigga treated me like some mid. The black jumpsuit I had on from Fashion Nova hugged my curves in all the right places. My hair was styled in a fishtail braid and perfectly complemented my outfit.

I didn't feel like wearing heels because I knew I had a long day ahead of me. Instead, I grabbed a pair of my clear slip-in sandals from the closet—I could never go wrong with a pair of those. I'd applied my lashes, did my brows, and put on some lip gloss too. I wasn't crazy about makeup because my natural beauty was already enough, and I loved not having to do too much to stand out.

I was shitting on bitches without even trying. Tay didn't give a damn, though, because he would still fuck off with a chick who had nothing on me. My mama always told me that coochie doesn't have a face, and I didn't really grasp that until I started fucking with Tay. Niggas would literally stick their dicks in anything. That was the main reason I barely gave that nigga any pussy now. He had one time to bring me home something from one of the nasty hoes he dealt with, and his mammy would be wearing his face on a t-shirt. I had never played those kinds of games and wasn't about to start.

The whole relationship with him was nearing an end, anyway. It wouldn't be long before I packed my shit and got on down. I just had to make sure my shit was in order first. Tay pretty much funded the lifestyle I lived, and I needed to at least be able to halfway maintain it before I dipped on his ass. Whenever I did decide to give that nigga a taste of his own medicine, Tay wouldn't know what hit him.

CHAPTER THREE

TAY

A nigga was sick and tired of dealing with the same bullshit day in and out. Amor was always down my throat about something, even when I was just chillin'. She always seemed to be looking for something as if she wanted a nigga to be doing her ass wrong. As the old saying goes, *if you go looking for something, you'll damn sure find it.* I hated that she wouldn't just leave well enough alone, but that was my girl for you.

True enough, Nina didn't have any business calling my fuckin' phone, knowing a nigga was at the crib, but Amor had no right to answer my phone in the first damn place. For me, that was always a no-go. I never touched her phone, even though I was the one paying the bill. Every time I thought we'd passed that stage, Amor showed me that I was wrong.

Some boundaries a person just shouldn't cross, and she'd done just that, only to get her feelings hurt in the process. Now, I had to listen to her bitch and complain about it for who knew how long. Amor was the type of female who would hold shit over a nigga's head for life, and I hated that with a passion.

I loved her to death, though, no matter what I went out in the streets and did with the next bitch. Amor was home, and my heart would always be with her. These other bitches knew they couldn't compete where they didn't compare. That's why they did dumb shit, like blowing up my phone in the middle of the night to purposely get under Amor's skin.

I knew who it was the entire time, but I had to play the shit cool. Nina was a bitch I'd been fucking with on the low for years. Normally, she played her role and kept shit cool. I didn't know what had gotten into the bitch or why she was acting brand new. I couldn't wait to pay her ass a visit and give her a piece of my mind. Little did she know, she was barking up the wrong tree.

Amor wasn't the one for her to be playing games with, and if she ever got wind of who Nina was, even I wouldn't be able to keep Amor off her ass. It may not have looked like it, but Amor had hands for days, and she didn't mind using them either. Amor was getting ready for one of her girl's days out, and I couldn't have been happier that she was going to be out of my hair. With her out of the house, I could move around and do what I wanted in peace.

"Where are you about to go, baby?" I quizzed.

"Me and Leilani are going to get pampered. We're probably going to catch a movie and have dinner somewhere, too," Amor informed.

"You need some money, or you straight?" I asked.

"Nigga, you know I need some money. I always need some money," Amor responded.

"Yo' ass do not need no money. You already have my credit card, but you know I got you, though. You know there is no limit to what you can have."

"Yeah, yeah, I know you do, and I know there isn't a limit. There better not be one, Tay," she sarcastically said.

"I love you, baby. I'll see you when you get back, okay? I have some business I need to handle, but I should be back before you," I let her know.

"Yeah, yeah. Do what you do and be safe while doing it."

"You know I will. I always do."

Amor was getting on my nerves with all that sarcastic bullshit she was throwing around. I knew I had at least a couple more days of her attitude and crazy ways because of the phone call. It was always something, man. I swear a nigga just couldn't win. I couldn't blame her for tripping, and I damn sure couldn't blame her for how she felt. If anything, I deserved for her to turn up some more. She handled the whole thing better than I expected her to. I didn't know if that was a good thing or a bad thing. Maybe she was just used to the shit, and if that was the case, that was even sadder.

I grabbed my pants and pulled out a stack of bills from the pockets. At that point, I didn't even care how much it was. I just knew it was enough to put a smile on her face and enough to take care of what she and her home girl had planned for the day. One thing about it, I may have been an ain't shit nigga, but I made sure my girl was always straight. Amor didn't want for a thing—if she so much as hinted at wanting something, it was hers. That was more than what I could say for most niggas.

These bitches knew that shit, too, and that's why they tried so desperately to take her spot. Amor deserved it, though, because she'd been with me through the toughest times. We went through the craziest shit, but still, I owed her the world. Besides, money was the least of my worries, and I always knew how to get some more if it were ever to become one. The way I saw it, there was too much money out there for any nigga to be broke.

Amor was down for a nigga, and even though she knew I was unfaithful to her, she never stepped out on me. I didn't know if she was dumb or loyal, but either way, I fucked with it. Amor wasn't one of those bitches who liked to get back at a nigga by going out and fucking another nigga. I loved the way she respected herself and her body, which is what caused me to fall for her in the first place. Amor was different. In fact, she'd always been, and I loved to brag about how good of a woman she was. I didn't have to worry about her being out there embarrassing me behind my back. Every nigga I knew wished they had a woman like mine.

I knew Amor respected me in my face and when I was nowhere around. She knew how to shut a nigga down and give him her ass to kiss. I'd seen her do it, and I'd heard how she read a nigga his rights plenty of times. Most niggas knew she belonged to me and to not even step to her on any bullshit, but of course, there were some dumb ass niggas who still tried.

No other nigga could ever say they had her; that would forever be one of my biggest flexes. For that, I could only respect her. I prayed she would stay by my side until I got my shit all the way together. I knew I had a good woman, and I damn sure didn't want to lose her. I already knew if she were to leave my ass, I wouldn't know what to do with myself. Amor was the glue that held me together. She was everything good inside me.

I played hard, as all men did, to portray a certain image, but I knew what the fuck I had. That's why I tried to keep what I did in the streets from touching my front door. Hoes didn't have any manners, though, and were always trying to make themselves relevant. The first time they didn't get their way, they tried to make problems with the main chick. I could never understand that shit. It was a dirty game, and for some reason, I still chose to be a player in it.

I couldn't stand Leilani because she always hopped from nigga to nigga. She and Amor were so different, and I never understood how they linked up and got so close in the first damn place. Leilani was the only female Amor had ever bought around me. When she wasn't out with her, she was in the house like I preferred her to be. The saying, *birds of a feather flock together,* didn't apply to those two. At least, I hoped not because I didn't even play those kinds of games. I could be out doing any and everything under the sun, but when it came to my woman, that shit was a no-go. Hell yeah, I could dish it, but I damn sure couldn't take it.

I took a shower, and afterward, I hopped in a fresh fit and paired it with the latest cherry 11s. I'd been dying to throw them joints on but never really got around to doing so. I had no idea what I wanted to get into. Some shit on the block required my attention, but I knew for a fact I had to pay Nina a visit. I had to check her ass about the dumb shit she'd decided to pull in person so she'd know not to ever pull any stunts like that again.

Nina was one of my favorites out of all the bitches on my roster. Until earlier that morning, I was under the impression that the two of us had an understanding, but she proved my ass wrong. I didn't even know her reason for doing the shit she did, but I was going to make it my business to find out. Clearly, Nina had lost her fuckin' mind. Either that or she'd forgotten her place, and I didn't mind putting her ass right back in it.

Out of all the bitches I dealt with, she was different, and we shared a different kind of connection. Of course, I was aware that she wanted more from me than I was able to give her, but never in a million years did I think she would get on straight bullshit and start playing phone games. I couldn't even stunt; I was disappointed in her. Nina was the one I didn't mind breaking bread with, but little did she know, she'd fucked all that up with the foul move she made. Acting on emotions could cost one everything, and she had to find that out the hard way. Thanks to her, Amor was on my ass like white on rice, and I didn't see her letting up anytime soon. I knew I had to come up with some exquisite shit to make it up to her or at least to try to get back on her good side.

Not on any cocky shit, but I was a fine ass nigga. I stood at 6'2" with a muscular frame, waves that could make a bitch seasick, and my hazel eyes were said to be hypnotizing. I had a perfect set of pearly whites, and when I smiled, I could make a female weak in the knees; at least, that's what the hoes always told me. My appearance was everything to me, and I always made sure my shit was up to par, unlike some niggas I knew.

I headed out the front door, hopped in my whip, and headed to Nina's crib. She stayed a good thirty minutes away from me. Normally, I wouldn't be up for the drive, but this day, it was necessary. I rolled a blunt and turned the radio all the way up. Finesse 2 Tymes' latest hit, "Overdose," blasted through the speakers as I got lost in my thoughts.

Deep down inside, I knew it was time for me to be a man and get my shit together, but at the same time, I wasn't ready to settle down and only be with one woman. Amor was everything I could have asked for in a partner, but for some reason, I still wasn't completely satisfied.

I decided to pop up on Nina without even letting her know I was coming. The plan was to catch her ass off guard. I had a key to her shit, so it wasn't like I had to wait for her to let me in. Gently, I eased the key inside the door and quietly opened it. At first glance, I saw that her son was asleep on the couch. I tiptoed toward her bedroom and saw her lying butt naked in bed, sleeping. It was a sight to see. Nina was fine, fine. I mean, top-of-the-line.

That girl was thick as fuck in all the right places. Her ass was out of this world and was one of the things that attracted me to her. That and her throat game, of course. Nina could suck a bullet out of a Glock that was on safety, if you know what I mean. She was my personal throat goat, and I hadn't run across a female who could do it better. Even her A-1 dick sucking skills wouldn't be enough to get her out of the trouble she was in with me, though.

"Nina, wake yo' ass up!" I said as I smacked her on her ass.

"Tay, what are you doing? Gone on, now. I'm trying to catch me a nap while Jay is sleeping. He has been doing the most all day," Nina whined.

"I don't give a fuck about none of that shit. Why the hell you pull that shit you pulled earlier?" I interrogated.

"I don't know what you're talking about, so please don't come in here starting this shit today," Nina said as she looked up at me with her pretty brown eyes.

"Nina, you a damn lie, and you know it. You know not to be blowing my phone up like that, and you should know better than to talk to my girl the way you did. I told your ass from the jump that none of the disrespect bullshit would be tolerated," I snapped.

"How you know it wasn't one of the other hoes you're sticking your dick in?" Nina nonchalantly quizzed.

I hated that nonchalant shit, and I had to catch myself from going upside her damn head.

"I know it was you because you're the only one who even knows my government name. The other hoes, as you call them, don't even know my real name is Dontavious. That's what gave your dumb ass away. Find you somebody to play with, Nina. Your ass is better off playing in traffic than playing with me," I warned.

"Well, first of all, nigga...."

"Well, first of all, what, Nina? Yeah, that's what the fuck I thought. Your dumb ass is good and caught," I snapped.

Nina couldn't even think of a comeback. She just sat there

squirming nervously on the bed. She knew her ass was good and caught, so there was no need for her to further deny the shit. I enjoyed watching her cave under pressure. It was crazy. Even though I was mad at her ass and came over with the intent to cut her off, my dick was hard as a rock just from looking at her. It was like her body was a work of art, and I was mesmerized by it. All I could think about was grabbing a fist full of her hair while I fed my dick to her.

I loved to watch her eat my big dick up, and I loved to watch her swallow my nut just as much. Nina was the definition of a freaky bitch, and hell, I figured since I was there, I might as well gone let her do what she did best. With the way Amor withheld the pussy from me, a nigga needed it because I damn sure had some pressure built up. I desperately needed to release that shit.

"Come and get big daddy right," I demanded.

Nina walked over to where I stood and dropped to her knees. She pulled down my Polo joggers and freed my dick from my Polo boxers. Seductively, she licked the tip of my shit and instantly made my ten inches disappear down her throat. If I didn't know any better, I'd think the bitch had just performed a magic trick. Nina sucked my dick like she had a point to prove. That shit was even sloppier than usual, and I didn't think that was even possible.

I forcefully pushed the back of her head, which caused her to gag on my dick. I didn't know why, but something about touching her tonsils did something to me. When I felt myself growing weak in the knees, I knew it was about that time. Nina started sucking my dick even faster, using her hands to really get the job done. I shot my load right down her throat, and she hungrily devoured every drop. That was the freaky shit that had a nigga stuck to her ass like glue.

"That's daddy's good girl," I complimented.

"Can I have some dick now, daddy?" Nina seductively asked.

"You know you can. Now, bend that ass over," I responded and gently slid inside her.

"Oh, shit, daddy! That shit feels so good. Yeesss! Dontavious, keep fucking me just like that!" Nina screamed out in pleasure.

"You like this shit, don't you? Keep on doing dumb shit, and this gon' be the last time you get it!" I said as I continued to deep stroke her.

The sound of her moaning was like music to my ears. The feeling of her wetness on my dick was something I couldn't seem to get enough of. Nina had some amazing pussy, and I loved the way she took the dick without running from it like most of the other bitches I fucked did. In her mind, it was her dick, and she damn sure knew what to do with it when it was in her possession. Nina dropped to her knees again and cleaned her juices off my dick with her tongue.

I picked her up as she straddled me and bounced her up and down on it. The only sound in the room was her ass clapping and macaroni noises. Momentarily, we'd both forgotten that Jay was in the front room sleeping until we were interrupted by him tapping on the door. That pussy was so good that I hated to climb out of it. Little man's timing couldn't have been worse. I cursed under my breath as I turned her loose, so she could tend to him.

"Mommy, what's wrong? Are you okay? Why are you screaming?" he asked.

"Mommy's fine, Jay. Dontavious and I were just playing a little game," Nina responded. "Mommy will be out in just a minute."

"Okay, Mommy. I don't like it when you play that game," he whined.

We couldn't help bursting into laughter because of the seriousness in lil' man's tone.

"I told your ass about making all that damn noise," I teased.

"Nigga, yo' dick was damn near touching my stomach. How did you expect me to be quiet?" Nina sarcastically asked.

"Whatever. Go get yourself cleaned up and tend to him."

"Okay. are you staying for a while?" Nina asked.

"Naw, I'm about to take a shower and head out. I got some business to handle on the block," I informed her.

"That's nothing new, Dontavious. Whatever. I guess I'll see you when I see you."

"Don't start that shit, Nina. I gave you what you wanted, so you should be good for a minute. I don't know why you choose to do this to yourself."

"What exactly am I doing to myself?"

"You ask me those dumb ass questions that you already know the answer to. Then, when I tell you the truth, you get all worked up over nothing. This is some everyday shit, yet you still continue to push the issue. I can't lay up all day, baby girl. My time is my money. Get you a broke nigga if that's what you're looking for."

"Yeah, you're right. But since you wanna be funny, I think you should know that you're about to be a daddy," Nina informed me with a smirk.

"What the fuck did you just say to me?" I asked, not believing what she'd just said.

"Nigga, you heard me the first time. I'm pregnant, and before you get to denying that it's yours, I'm a hundred percent sure you're the father. I haven't been fucking nobody but you."

"Bitch, I know damn well you don't expect me to believe that shit. We gon' get to the bottom of this shit later. I've been careful as fuck with you. I don't need this bullshit right now," I said as I grabbed my keys off the table and headed to the front door.

It may have come off as selfish and inconsiderate for me to just up and leave after Nina delivered what she assumed was good news, but at that moment, the only thing I could think about was getting the fuck out of there. A part of me didn't believe she was pregnant in the first place. That was a line females resorted to when they were about to lose a nigga. And if she did happen to be pregnant, that didn't guarantee the baby belonged to me. For all I knew, that could have been anybody's baby.

Nina and I had a real good time whenever we linked, but I didn't put shit past her. Hell, she was probably bouncing up and down on another nigga's dick when mine wasn't available to her. I mean, that shit was only right. Hell, after all, it wasn't like she belonged to me, and I damn sure didn't belong to her. So, she owed my black ass no loyalty. I couldn't care less about who she gave her pussy to. Long as my girl wasn't giving my pussy away, that was all that mattered. Amor was the only female who could make me catch a case behind her.

The last thing I needed to do was to give my girl something else to hold over my head. Cheating on her was one thing, but to go out and have a baby by a bitch was pushing it. Stepping out on Amor was nothing new to either of us, but I knew if Nina was indeed pregnant by me, it would be the end of my relationship. Hell, I couldn't even blame Amor for not wanting shit else to do with me.

In just a few hours' time, my day had gone from bad to even worse. I imagined Nina must have been having a field day with that shit. Although I thought I knew her, the truth of the matter was, I didn't know what to expect from her anymore. If she was bold enough to play phone games, there was no telling what else she would do. Obviously, her being pregnant made her feel like she had power over me. Maybe she did, at least for the moment. I couldn't even lie; a nigga felt defeated. I didn't know if I was coming or going.

A nigga didn't have any kids and honestly never even wanted any. But if the shit were to happen, I always imagined Amor being the mother of my seeds. At least I had real love for her, and she wasn't just a random female I was dicking down. Nina was cool and all, but I couldn't see myself creating life with her, nor could I see myself having to deal with her for the rest of my life. Having a child was permanent and meant I'd have to deal with her until my child was old enough that we wouldn't have to interact with each other through Nina.

The more I thought about the shit, the angrier I became. I'd fucked up big time, and the only one I could blame for the entire situation was me. There was no reason for me to step out on Amor, and now that I thought about it, doing so without using protection was even crazier. I quickly found myself in a situation I swore I'd never be in. There was no way in hell I'd managed to slip up like that. I got so comfortable with Nina that I stopped strapping up and fell for that whole her being on birth control and not being able to get pregnant lie.

Of course, if it turned out to be my baby, I would take care of it. I would never be a deadbeat type of nigga under any circumstances. I didn't want to get ahead of myself and start claiming some shit without knowing the facts first, though. A bitch could tell me anything, but I needed to see that shit in black and white. Until I had proof, as far as I was concerned, I wasn't the father. If Nina decided to fight me on getting the paternity test done, then she would have to deal with the aftermath on her own. If she wanted to raise a child without my assistance, I would let her have that.

I struggled with what I wanted to do next. Amor deserved

to hear the news from me; the last thing I wanted was for her to be blindsided. I also couldn't risk letting Nina get to her before I got around to telling her myself. All bets would be off if that were to happen. I was fucked either way, and no matter what I decided to do, I couldn't win. Amor would be pissed whenever I decided to tell her the fucked-up news. All I could do was hope and pray that God would get my black ass out of the mess that I'd foolishly gotten myself into. I didn't deserve it —that I knew—but I still hoped for a miracle. I needed Nina to be on chill until she delivered the baby, and we could figure the rest out afterward.

CHAPTER FOUR

AMOR

I was still mad as fuck about the bitch calling Tay's phone, but I wasn't mad enough to not spend that nigga's money. When I made it to the car, I unfolded the money he had given me and counted fifteen crisp hundred-dollar bills. He was in a very generous mood for a nigga who had just gotten caught up in the middle of some bullshit. I would resume being mad at him once I'd gone shopping and spent every dime he'd given to me. I called Leilani again to let her know I was en route to her. Leilani was never on time for anything, and I didn't feel like playing the waiting game with her.

Some drinks were desperately needed, and I couldn't wait to tell her the latest Tay drama. Leilani hated Tay's ass with a passion, and I couldn't blame her one bit. That was just how we were with each other. Leilani was overprotective of me and my feelings as I was hers. To my surprise, when I pulled up to get her, she was already outside waiting for me. I guess something about hearing the word shopping made her put some pep in her step. Whatever the case, I was glad not to have to sit outside and wait twenty minutes for her as I normally would have to do.

"Hey, bitch!" she greeted as she got into the car.

"Hey, hoe! You look cute as fuck," I complimented.

"Thanks, boo. So do you. What's the move for the day?" Leilani quizzed while applying her lip gloss.

"A little retail therapy, of course, and we have to get some drinks. My nerves are shot, girl," I replied.

"I don't like the sound of that. What the fuck has this nigga done to you now, Amor?"

"Girl, it's a long story. Let me get a drink or two in me before we get to all of that."

"Damn, it's that bad, huh?" Leilani quizzed.

"Yep, but then again, when it comes to Tay, nothing that nigga does even surprises me anymore. I'm not even mad at him. I'm just looking at him sideways like, damn, I thought you were realer than that. You know?"

"Damn, that's deep, friend. You know I won't ever tell you to leave his ass because I know how you feel about him. You're a good person, and you deserve so much better. All I know is when you leave his ass, he's going to be on suicide watch. I'm not saying this just because you're my best friend, but you're not the kind of female a nigga runs across twice," Leilani expressed.

"Dang, girl, you gon' make a thug cry over here with all that sentimental shit. I appreciate you adjusting my crown, though. I couldn't agree with you more. If anything, that nigga should be holding on to me with both hands. But he'll realize what he had when I'm no longer his."

"Facts, and it's sad that it has to come down to that before niggas can get their shit together."

"Yes, it is, Lei, but anyway, enough about that for now. What do you wanna do first? I want to go and get a silk press and my nails done," I said.

"Now, you know I'm down for both of those. These ends need some serious attention, and so do these nails. I've been trying to get to the nail shop all week to no avail," Leilani responded as she looked down at her nails and shook her head.

"Okay, I got you. By the way, everything is on me today," I informed her with a smile.

"Bitch, what? Am I being punked or something?" Leilani teased.

"Not at all. You can thank Tay and his bullshit for that. You know when a nigga is guilty, there's no limit to what they will do or how much money they will dish out."

"I'm sorry that nigga had you fucked up, friend, but I'm not even mad at a girl's day on his trifling ass."

"My sentiments exactly, Lei. I'm not even tripping. I just want to make the best of the day and spend that nigga's money."

"Well, we gon' get your mind off that shit today. You already know where I stand when it comes to that nigga, anyway. I'm forever screaming fuck him," Leilani pointed out.

"You already know I know that shit. But, yes, I'm not even trying to think about that nonsense right now," I responded.

We decided to go to the salon downtown. I loved the vibes and the hospitality they showed to their clients. I got lost in my thoughts as the lady massaged my scalp. When she was done washing and conditioning my hair, she sat me under the dryer and then started on Leilani's head. I took out my phone and began to browse through my social media accounts. I went from TikTok to Twitter and ended up on Facebook, which I always found to be the most entertaining. Bitches on that app would literally sell their souls in exchange for likes and comments.

I was one of those women who rarely posted. Now and then, I would get on to update my profile picture, and that was about it. I did enjoy being in everyone else's business and laughing at them for making a damn fool of themselves, though. I would never! If anything, I took my losses in private, especially when I knew I wasn't going to leave the nigga alone, but that was just me. I didn't see how others put themselves in a position to be publicly humiliated.

After I had sipped the latest social media tea, one of the other hairdressers motioned for me to come to their work area, and she finished my hair. She worked a miracle on my hair, and I was very much pleased when I looked in the mirror and saw the results. My hair had grown out so much, but I would never have realized it had I not come in to get the silk press because I wore protective styles and didn't rock my natural hair as much as I should have. The maintenance of dealing with my hair was way too time consuming, or maybe I was just lazy; whatever the case, it was a hard no for me. I gave myself a good two weeks tops before I would get some weave sewed in or another hairstyle.

I looked over to where my friend was sitting, and I couldn't help but admire how beautiful she was. Leilani's hair was way longer than mine, and she was the opposite of me. Weave couldn't touch her head, and she did a good job maintaining her natural hair.

"Your hair is so pretty, friend," Leilani complimented as she walked over to me.

"Yours is too, and it has gotten long as hell," I responded.

"Bitch, you already know ain't no baldheaded shit going on over here," Leilani teased as she swung her hair from side to side.

"No baldheaded shit whatsoever," I agreed.

"I'm starving, Amor. Where are we going to eat?" Leilani quizzed.

"There's this new spot downtown called 122 that everyone has been bragging about. You want to check it out?" I asked.

"Hell yeah, we can check it out. You know I'm always down to try new things and new foods."

"I forgot who I was talking to for a minute. Let me go take care of the bill, and we can go," I said.

After paying and generously tipping the ladies who did our hair, we headed for the car. I didn't have much of an appetite because the altercation with Tay from earlier that day was still embedded in my head, but I knew I had to eat something if I wanted to drink. Supposedly, 122 had some of the best drinks, and I was damn sure ready to take a few of them down. I hoped that by the time I made it home, Tay would be already asleep. Or better yet, not home at all. He was known for late nights and sometimes not coming home at all.

Now, I could truly say I gave no fucks whether he did or not. Being around him would only lead to us arguing and fighting. I wasn't in the mood to go back and forth with his ass, especially since the truth was nowhere in him. I could handle the truth, even if it hurt my feelings; it was being lied to that triggered my inner craziness. Nothing sat right about a nigga lying to me right in my face while looking me dead in my eyes.

Tay showed no remorse, and that was an even bigger issue. The worst kind of nigga to deal with was one who never held themselves accountable for their wrongdoings. That shit started to get old real fast.

Thirty minutes later, we pulled up at 122. I could look at it and tell that the vibe would be chill. It was packed, and I could barely find an available parking spot. I hated crowds, but I knew Leilani wouldn't let me change my mind about eating there. So, I sucked it up, parked, and we went inside. It wasn't like the normal chill spots we went to in the hood. The vibe was laid back for the grown and sexy crowd. It wasn't the type of spot where any drama would pop off, and I loved the fact that they played R&B music.

Once we were seated, we rocked back and forth in our seats and sang along to damn near every song they played. Before long, our waitress came to take our food and drink orders. She quickly came back with our drinks. I downed the Hennything Possible I'd ordered and sent for a refill. Leilani wasn't much of a drinker, so she babysat the Strawberry Patrón Splash she'd ordered. A few sips in, and I could already tell that sis was feeling herself.

Twenty minutes later, our waitress came back with our food. I ordered the fish and grits meal while Leilani's greedy ass ordered lamb chops and southern baked mac and cheese. I couldn't even lie; everything was delicious. For the first time in history, I had no complaints about anything. From the food to the customer service, everything was top-tier. Judging by the way Leilani's plate looked, I knew she was satisfied as well. I glanced over the menu for something else to drink and couldn't help but be intrigued when I saw the drinks named after celebrities like Betty Wright, Johnnie Taylor, and Ike&Tina. I'd never heard of anything like those drinks before and had to give the establishment props for its uniqueness.

"Can I get you ladies anything else?" the waitress asked as she removed our plates from the table.

"Yes, I would like to try the Ike&Tina," I requested, hoping the drink would whoop my ass like Ike did Tina's. When I did get home, all I wanted to do was go the fuck to sleep.

"And I guess I'll try the Betty Wright," Leilani hesitantly added.

"Okay. I'll be right back with your drinks. Let me know if you need anything else," she said before she left our table.

"Damn, bitch, are you going to tell me what happened with Tay or not?" Leilani asked.

"Bitch, I was trying not to even revisit the shit, but some bitch was blowing his phone up this morning. Me being me, I went in the bathroom and answered his phone," I confided.

"What? What did the hoe say? Do we need to go whoop this bitch?" Leilani interrogated.

"Girl, you wouldn't believe this shit, but this bitch had the nerve to ask me who the fuck I was and why the fuck I was answering her man's phone," I recalled. "My whooping ass days are over, especially over a nigga who doesn't want to be kept."

"I swear these hoes are so bold these days, and it's because niggas have them feeling themselves. Did she tell you who she was, though? Because we can go beat her ass," Leilani expressed.

That bitch was always on go, and that was one of the things I loved most about her.

"That's exactly what it is. These women act like that because he gives them a reason to. True enough, I went off on her ass because I was pissed the fuck off, but my real issue lies with Tay. Naw, that bitch didn't tell me who she was, but I told her my man was asleep and to stop calling his damn phone."

"Hmph, and how did he lie himself out of that one?"

"Bitch, the nigga had the nerve to tell me it was somebody playing on his damn phone. He won't even own up to his shit. I'm over him at this point. But I know whoever the bitch was, she wasn't lying on him. She called him by his government name and all. So, there was no way she could have been playing on the phone," I vented.

"I think you need a little vacation from here. My boo is

gifting me a trip to San Francisco for my birthday, and I think you should come. You have less than two weeks to decide if you wanna go or not. I already have the tickets, and if you don't want to go, I'll ask someone else."

"Bitch, you don't have to ask me twice. I've never been to Cali before, and I heard there were some fine ass, rich ass men there too," I beamed. "Who else were you going to ask to tag along anyway, friendly hoe?"

"Yeah, all of that. That's right up my alley too. Might fuck around and not even come back home," Leilani joked.

"I'm geeked. I finally have something to look forward to. I get so tired of sitting in that damn house, looking at four walls all day while Tay's trifling ass is out doing God knows what or who."

"Don't even worry, my girl. We're going to turn you all the way up. So, go ahead and get your wardrobe together. We gotta be on our bad bitch shit."

"I'm always on my bad bitch shit, so you didn't even have to say all that," I sarcastically responded.

"Yeah, you're right! I have no idea what I'm wearing. We should have gone to the mall before we went to have drinks, Amor."

"It's all good, boo. We can always go tomorrow."

"Okay, that sounds good to me. I'll see you tomorrow. Go home and get you some rest. And try not to let that man get under your skin. He's not even worth you getting all worked up over."

"I know, boo. I'm okay now. I'm not even worried about it because it's going to be whatever it's going to be, and that nigga gon' do whatever the fuck he wanna do. In the meantime, I'll be working on getting my own shit and letting him do him in peace," I verbalized.

"Now that's what I love to hear. I know you've probably been putting money to the side for a rainy day, right?"

"Of course I have. Every chance I get, I stash some money to the side. Most of the time, whatever he puts in my hands, I put in my savings account. I know I have enough to pay the first month's rent and deposit and a few months of rent in advance. One thing about Tay, though, he won't ever leave me in a fucked-up position, especially when he knows he's the reason I'm leaving," I explained.

"I know you want to believe that, friend, but these niggas ain't shit, and they will switch up on you in a heartbeat. Especially if you're not doing what they want you to do," Leilani countered.

"It's all good, Lei. I'll cross that bridge when I get there."

"You're the smartest, strongest woman I know, so I have no doubt that you got shit covered, Amor."

"Thanks for the vote of confidence, friend."

"Anytime, girl. That's what I'm here for," Leilani reminded me.

By the time we left 122, we both were so fucked up that we decided to take it in. The time spent with Leilani was much needed, but I still didn't feel any better about the whole Tay situation. I could barely stand up, and I had no damn business getting behind the wheel and operating a car. After I dropped Leilani off and made sure she got in the house safely, I headed straight home. I prayed that I wouldn't get pulled over on the way there because drunk driving wouldn't look good on my clean record.

I turned up the radio and blasted Jazmine Sullivan's song "Hurt Me So Good" all the way home. She did her shit with that song, and I was sure every woman in the world could relate to the words. *I hope that I find the strength, so I let go, hey, 'cause you got a hold on my mental. Why I stick beside him, so deceitful boy, you're lethal.* I sang along with her because that part of the song hit home more than anything else she said. I was more in my feelings than I previously was when I pulled into my driveway. Slow jams and liquor never mixed. I knew that firsthand and still did the same dumb ass shit every time I got drunk.

"What the fuck is this nigga doing here?" I asked myself.

I rolled my eyes so hard that I thought they were going to pop out of my head when I noticed Tay's car parked in the driveway. He was the last person I wanted to see. I sat in the car and contemplated leaving but decided to just go inside. In my condition, I wouldn't have made it far, anyway. I wondered what had done the trick, the Hennythings Possible or the Ike and Tina. One of the two whooped my ass, for sure.

I was feeling damn good, and normally, I would have wanted to be dicked down, but I wouldn't have dared let Tay touch me. He didn't deserve to swim inside my wetness, anyway. I was thankful for my toy collection because I was damn sure going to put it to use. I didn't know what it was about alcohol, but the shit went right to my kitty.

When I walked into the house, the first thing I saw was Tay passed out on the couch. I tip-toed past the living room area and up the stairs that led to the bedroom.

I started a hot bubble bath, grabbed one of my rose sex toys, and eased into the bathtub. In another dimension, I placed the toy on the third setting and let it do whatever the hell it did to me. I couldn't control my moans as I continuously climaxed. Whoever invented that toy was on to something because Tay had never made my body react in such a manner. I heard footsteps, and when the bathroom door slowly opened, I knew Tay was watching me get off, but I didn't care. I got even more into it and dramatically moaned.

It took everything in me not to laugh out loud when the

nigga walked into the bathroom with his rock-hard manhood in his hands. Tay's third leg standing at attention was a beautiful sight to see—I couldn't even lie—but I wasn't fuckin' with it, not even the slightest. I had to stand for something because I damn sure wasn't about to fall for anything.

"It sounded like you were in need of my assistance, baby," he had the nerve to utter.

"First of all, I'm already done, and secondly, you never thought I was about to let you get on me," I snapped.

"Amor, please. You know you want some of daddy's good dick," Tay boasted.

"Naw, nigga, I don't. How about you go fuck the bitch who called your phone this morning? I mean, she did say you were her man." I shrugged and climbed out of the tub.

I wrapped a towel around my dripping wet body and went into the bedroom to find some night clothes to slip into. Once I found one of my comfortable pajama sets, I slipped it on after I dried off. I could tell by the way Tay walked around the house, slamming doors and talking shit under his breath, that he was pissed at me. Once again, I had to fight back my laughter because the way he acted was quite humorous.

As bad as I wanted to grant him access to my body and allow him to do the most ungodly things to me, I couldn't stop thinking about what that bitch said. I wouldn't be satisfied until I found out whether there was any truth to it or not. I didn't know where to start when it came to investigating the situation, but I had to get to the bottom of it once and for all.

If I knew one thing about irrelevant bitches, it was that they would do anything to make themselves known. All I had to do was sit pretty and wait patiently. The next time Tay pissed her ass off, she would be back on her messy shit and try to cause confusion where he laid his head. I'd never wanted a bitch to come to me as a woman so badly in my life. I was certain he'd already warned her not to make that move because I wasn't shit to play with. But, then again, from how rowdy she'd gotten over the phone, she probably wasn't the type of bitch that he could just bark out orders to.

CHAPTER FIVE

NINA

A week and three days had gone by since the last time I'd seen Dontavious. It wasn't like him to not come around or not answer my phone calls, and I couldn't even stunt. It was getting the best of me. Granted, I knew he was upset with me, but that still didn't give him the right to act so cold. Maybe I was wrong for blowing his phone up in the wee hours of the morning, knowing he was home with his bitch, but at that time, I didn't care. I needed him to know I was pregnant with his baby.

As soon as those two lines popped up on that test, I needed to share my exciting news with him. After all, I didn't nut in myself and get pregnant—that was all on him. Never in a million years did I expect her to pick up his phone. That shit floored me, and when she had the nerve to get slick with me, I lost the little sense I had.

I met Dontavious one night at my job. At the time, I was a stripper—an occupation I'd never been proud of. But as a single mother, I had to do what I had to do. The money flow was fast and easy. I was able to more than carry my weight by dancing at the club for a few hours a night. From the first time I laid eyes on Dontavious, I knew I had to have him. I got everything I wanted, and getting with him wasn't any different. Dontavious made sure to make his presence known any time he was in the building. He went out of his way to request me for table dances, and we had even ventured off to the private rooms a few times. As a matter of fact, the first time I gave him the pussy was in one of those rooms.

All he was looking for was a dance and some conversation, but I had something else in mind. From then on, his ass was hooked. He was like a fish, and my pussy was the bait. Even then, he made sure to let me know he was in a serious relationship. I never took him seriously when he said it because his actions said something totally different. I wasn't thrilled about dealing with a nigga who had a bitch at home, but the more we were around each other, the harder I found it to let go.

Aside from the bomb ass sex we had, Dontavious and I had a crazy vibe. He was there for me in ways no other man had ever been, and he understood me. I could confide in him about any and everything, and he never judged me. It wasn't long before he gave me an ultimatum; either I quit my job, or he would quit dealing with me. Clearly, I chose him. I was tired of that damn job, anyway. The niggas were way too damn disrespectful, and the time spent dancing was cutting into the time I could have been spending with my son.

We weren't exclusive or anything of that nature, but he didn't want everyone to have access to what he had access to, and I could respect that. With the way he was laying the pipe and providing for me, there wasn't too much I would disagree with him about. Dontavious had me right where he wanted me, and he knew it. Letting him know how bad I had it for him was probably one of the biggest mistakes I'd made.

During the three years I had dealt with Dontavious, I'd

heard all the crazy stories about Amor and the many asses she'd whooped behind him. That shit was neither here nor there with me because I wasn't one of those bitches, and I was willing to bet money that she couldn't fuck with me. If it was ever to come down to it, I would be the one to give her ass a run for her money.

I knew I had no right to act the way I acted about a man who didn't belong to me, but I couldn't help it. When I say I loved that nigga, flaws and all, I meant just that. As far as I was concerned, he was just as much my man as he was that bitch's.

I walked into the situation fully aware of what I was getting myself into. It wasn't like I didn't know he was attached to another female or like he'd lied to me or sugar-coated anything about his home life. Amor's presence had always been very much known, and he always spoke so highly of her. So much so that it made me sick to my stomach most of the time. His definition of love was always sketchy to me because a man in love wouldn't do all the hurtful shit he did to her. But what did I know? I damn sure couldn't judge her when I was standing in line, waiting to take her place in his life.

I knew I was crazy, and he wouldn't treat me any better. But I wanted what I wanted, and what I wanted happened to be Dontavious. I didn't know why I assumed I could be the one to make him change his distasteful ways. In his eyes, she could do no wrong and was the epitome of perfection, which made no sense at all because he was always knee-deep in my pussy. I should have known then that something was wrong with his ass, but I just couldn't let him go.

That nigga was good to me, and the way he dicked me down was even better. No man had ever handled me like he did, and in my twenty-six years, I'd never been fucked or sucked the way he fucked and sucked me. I understood why Amor stayed and accepted the shit he dished out. I could just imagine the kind of dick he was giving out at home. Just the thought of him fucking her made me livid. Although I knew what our situation was, I wanted more, and I couldn't help it.

That man was going to be mine, and I wouldn't be satisfied until he was. I wasn't ever letting up, and I let him know that shit every chance I got. I wasn't one who he would just pick up and put down when he felt like it. If he thought I was, he was in for a very rude awakening.

Getting pregnant wasn't planned at all. Hell, I was just as surprised as Dontavious was. But, still, I hoped it would work out in my favor. I didn't feel like he would just leave me with a baby to raise alone, and I knew if Amor found out I was pregnant with her man's baby, she would be ready to leave his black ass high and dry. At least, that's what I hoped. Babies were always the deal breakers. A bitch would stay with a nigga through everything except him having a baby on her. One would have to be a strong bitch to ride with a nigga through all of that.

As crazy as I was, I knew I couldn't do it and wouldn't even attempt to. I would straight show a nigga the door before I played stepmother to another bitch's child. I was interrupted from my thoughts by my son walking through my bedroom door.

"Mommy, I'm ready to eat. Eat now, Mommy," Jay whined.

"Okay, baby, we're about to find something to eat in just a few minutes," I responded.

Jay was five years old, and dealing with him and his tantrums made me wonder how the hell I would be able to deal with two children running around, causing havoc. I vowed to be a one child having female for the rest of my life, but somehow, I'd gotten caught slipping. Because of how Dontavious interacted with my son, I knew without a shadow of a doubt that he would be an amazing father. When

Dontavious and I started fooling around, Jay had just turned two. He was so selfless when it came to Jay, and I loved everything about the bond the two of them shared.

Jay's sperm donor was a piece of shit, so he hadn't seen much of him since he'd been in the world. I hated that my son had to go through the whole stage of feeling unwanted, and I thanked God for Dontavious because he'd more than filled that void. DNA didn't mean a damn thing. According to my son, Dontavious was his daddy, and I wouldn't have had it any other way. No matter how bad things were between us, he always came through for my son, which resulted in me loving him even more. As a mother, the way to my heart was through my son.

The fact that Dontavious acted like he was so disappointed that we were about to be parents had me thrown completely off. I wasn't exactly jumping for joy when I found out the news myself, but damn, he could have shown a little enthusiasm. I didn't know what I expected, but I thought he would have been thrilled that he was about to have his first child, but obviously, it didn't matter to him. I wondered if Amor had been the one knocked up, would he have had a different reaction?

I had to find a way to get through to him. He was pissed at me for interfering with his home life, and I honestly couldn't blame him for tripping. I'd crossed the line, which I imagined was like a slap in the face to him because we'd always been big on boundaries and respect. He had me fucked up, and he knew it.

The only time I jumped out of character was when he played me like a damn fool. In my feelings was the worst place for me to be, and that's why I tried to stay out of them. That was impossible to do when dealing with the nigga I was dealing with, though. He always found a way to take me there, and sometimes, I believed he did so on purpose. I think it made the nigga's dick hard to see me all worked up and acting a fool with him. Yeah, it had to because it never failed; we ended up fucking like crazy each time I turned up on his ass. Dontavious liked crazy shit like that, even though he claimed not to like drama.

That shit was cool in the beginning stages, but once I caught feelings, it became harder and harder to deal with. I often wondered why I put up with the shit I accepted. It wasn't like I was an ugly bitch. I was fine as wine and could have easily had any nigga I wanted. If a nigga looked, that nigga could've been took. Niggas in the hood loved them a thick, redbone bitch, and that was me. The heart wanted what it wanted, though. My situation was living proof of that statement.

Dontavious made it clear that he would never leave what he had at home, but I wanted it all. I didn't want him coming over just to fuck on me and then dip. I saw the two of us being so much more than what we were. In time, I knew he would see it too. I could be just as good of a woman as Amor was to him. Then again, if that bitch was so top-tier, why was he out doing all the shit he was doing behind her back? The math wasn't mathing to me, but he didn't want to hear shit, period, when it came to her.

After I prepared lunch for my son and got him situated, I grabbed my phone and dialed Dontavious's number, only to once again be sent to voicemail. I couldn't believe the type of time the nigga was on. Clearly, he wanted me to pop up on his ass since he chose to avoid contact with me. I knew everything about that nigga, including where he and his girl laid their heads. Even Dontavious didn't know I knew all the shit that I did. I often rode by his spot, just to make sure he was where he said he was and not out with another bitch. That nigga was always on some bullshit, and just like Amor, I had to whoop some ass here and there when I noticed my face was being played in. It was sad as fuck the shit women would endure just to say they had a man, or in my case, a piece of a man.

Knowing I deserved better was one thing, but having the nerve to walk away was completely different. Leaving him was close to impossible. Love was a drug, and I found myself about to overdose. The whole side chick title was nothing new to me because I'd had my fair of situation-ships. The only difference this time was that I'd broken the first rule. The first rule was to never FEEL, and Dontavious happened to have me deep in my feelings.

Never would I have thought that I'd be head over heels in love with someone else's man. A nigga who probably didn't even love me. Good treatment didn't equate to being loved. So, I'd never go around bragging like the nigga loved me just because he would do whatever for me. I wasn't naïve by a long shot, and I could always read between the lines. Either way, Dontavious was going to be stuck with me for life, so we had to make the best out of a complicated situation.

After going back and forth with myself for the longest, I eventually said fuck it. I put Jay in the car and carefully fastened his seatbelt around him. I had decided to pop up on Dontavious wherever he was. The last thing I wanted was to go to his house, but he left me no other choice. He was going to hear what I had to say one way or the other; he owed me that much. He wasn't about to just run off on me and leave me alone with a baby to raise. When it came to my feelings, I didn't give a fuck. We could all be booked and processed.

I stopped by my sister's apartment on the way there to drop Jay off. I couldn't have him around me if some drama popped off. My visit to their house didn't have a damn thing to do with Amor, but of course, I knew she would come at me sideways again. I could be as rachet as they came. However, I would never let my son see that side of me. To him, I could no wrong, and I wanted to keep that image he had of me for a long time.

When I pulled into the apartment complex, my sister and her kids were already outside. As Jay got out of the car and walked toward the other kids, my sister made her way over. I rolled the window down to see what she wanted. I wasn't in the mood for her shit today. My sister, Esha, was always begging or wanting to borrow some money until her payday, which never came around. That bitch owed me so much money that I'd lost count. I made it my business to drop my son off to her every chance I got, whether I needed to or not. Hell, she was going to pay me back one way or another.

"Esha, what do you want? I'm telling your ass now. I don't have any money, so don't even ask me for any."

"Bitch, I don't need any money. I came to see what you were up to. You normally don't just drop my nephew off without calling first. I can see it all in your face that you got hell inside you," Esha expressed.

"You might be right about that. I'm headed to Dontavious's house," I nonchalantly informed her.

"You mean the same house he shares with his girl?" Esha questioned.

"Yes, that same house. I mean, he's not answering my calls or responding to my texts. That means he wants to see me in person, right?" I quizzed.

"Nina, don't go over there starting shit. You know you are dead ass wrong for even thinking about going over them folks' house on bullshit. We don't have any money to get your dick dumb ass out of jail either, so don't even call Mama or me."

"Look, Esha, please leave me alone and mind your own damn business. I got this! And I would never call your broke ass for money. You still owe me, remember? Jay has already eaten, so he should be good until I get back. I won't be long," I said and put the car in reverse, then pulled off before she could even respond.

Of course, Esha was right, but I hated for someone to be all in my business, trying to tell me right from wrong, especially when they didn't have room to talk. The way I looked at it, I wasn't doing shit that anyone else hadn't done before. I wouldn't be the first or the last bitch to knowingly be a nigga's sidepiece. Even Esha had been one before. The only difference was she left her situation empty-handed, but I was having shit my way.

One thing a bitch couldn't say was that my nigga didn't come through for me because he always did, at least until I decided to mess up our little arrangement. Tay not fucking with me on the financial tip was his way of letting me know he was done with me, I guess. I wasn't about to just roll over and take that shit lying down, though. Dontavious had to see me. There was no way for him to get around it.

I hadn't received a CashApp or a Chime transfer since the incident occurred, but I wasn't tripping. It wasn't like I was a broke bitch. I was always going to make sure I was straight; I owed that much to my child. What a nigga did for me was only a plus. My mind was in overdrive the entire drive to Dontavious's house. What I was about to do was risky business, and one of two things would happen behind it. I was either going to lose my man for good, or he would finally open his eyes and realize what had been standing right in front of him all along.

I already knew Amor wouldn't take my just showing up on her front doorstep lightly, but I had some shit I needed to get off my chest. Hopefully, I wouldn't have to have a round with her feisty ass, but I was almost certain Dontavious wouldn't let that happen. He didn't entertain drama and wouldn't like us fighting because of him. For all I knew, maybe she wouldn't even be home, which would defeat the purpose of going in the first place. That shit was long overdue, and it was time for her to know who the other woman in his life was. I had my days, and I had some fucked up ways, but I was a good ass woman. I could've been an even better one to him if he hadn't been so quick to shut down the idea of us being more.

Now that I was carrying that nigga's seed, they both had a long ass time to deal with me, and how easy of a task it would be, I would leave up to them. I really didn't want any smoke with sis, but I refused to be silenced. It was time that I finally be heard. Dontavious had his fun for long enough. So many times, I'd asked him to handle the shit, so since he couldn't, I decided to make it easier on him. He didn't have to introduce me because I was about to make my own dramatic introduction.

Dontavious wasn't to be fucked with, and I knew his ass could get a little crazy, but hell, I wasn't to be fucked with either. The moment he chose to ignore me and make me feel like my feelings weren't valid, the little respect I had for him went out the window.

I was done playing by his rules. It was time he played by mine for a change. No matter how he felt about it, the ending would be the same. I would get what I wanted, regardless.

CHAPTER SIX

AMOR

"So, you just gon' leave and not tell a nigga where you going, Amor?" Tay whined like a little ass boy.

"Nigga, I'm grown as fuck. I don't have to tell you anything. All you need to know is that I'm going to help Lei celebrate her birthday. You should be able to rest easy knowing that I'm not on the kind of bullshit you are," I informed him.

"That's all your stubborn ass had to say in the first place. Tell Lei I said happy birthday, and I want you to enjoy yourself, baby. Here, take this bread, and you already have the card. You know it ain't no limit to what you can have."

"Thanks, Tay. I'll tell her, and thanks for making sure I'm good. I'll be home in a few days. I would tell you to behave yourself, but we both know that's not going to happen."

"Damn, baby, you should have more faith in your man than that," Tay expressed, acting offended.

"Nigga, please. I know my man, and that's exactly why I said what the fuck I said. It's all good, though."

"We're not going to start that this morning. Let me take your luggage to the car."

"I guess you can do that," I responded as I rolled my eyes. The nigga was being way too nice. I knew firsthand that it was a result of guilt. I had no idea what he'd done, but I knew it wouldn't be long before whatever it was came to light. God didn't play about me, and he always put things right in front of me. Most of the time, I didn't even have to go looking for shit. I vowed never to be that type of woman again. Besides, as more days went by, the less I was fazed by any of it. I had a few tricks up my sleeves, and if I played my cards right, I would be out of that nigga's life before he even realized I was gone. By the time he did, it would be way too late.

I'd purposely decided not to tell him that I was going somewhere with Leilani, just to ruffle his feathers. Besides the occasional girl's night out, I was quite the homebody and never went anywhere. That was right up Tay's alley because it gave him a free pass to do what he wanted out in the streets without me catching him. That was also how he knew his goodies weren't being tampered with while he was out doing dirt with other bitches. I wanted that nigga's mind to wonder about my activities while I was gone. My phone wouldn't be used at all unless I wanted to upload some pics on social media.

My not answering the phone for him was sure to break him down. Lucky for him, I didn't believe in using my body to get some get back. It never even crossed my mind to go out and fuck a random nigga, all because I was mad at my nigga. That was a popular wave that I just couldn't see myself riding. I valued my body, and a man not knowing my worth wouldn't make me lose my own value. I knew so many females who'd upped the score on their body count, only for the niggas they wanted to hurt to not give one lovely fuck.

After Tay placed my bags in the car, I drove off without saying another word to him. I owed it to myself and Leilani to have a good time. I couldn't remember the last time I'd taken a trip anywhere, and I felt like it was time for me to live a little instead of just existing. I didn't even plan to mention Tay's name while we were away on the birthday trip. Leilani wouldn't want to hear shit about him, anyway. The weekend was about my friend and my friend only. I couldn't wait until we touched down in Cali, so I could blow a bag on her.

I never minded breaking the bank when it came to her because she deserved it and would never hesitate to do the same for me in return. Everything about our friendship was mutual; never were there any forced interactions or uncomfortable scenarios. I never had to question her loyalty, and for that reason, I fucked with her the long way.

When I made it to Leilani's, I parked in the garage as I was instructed. Her boo, Elijah, was there, ready to drive us to the airport. I didn't know too much about him, nor had I really been around him, but from how Leilani bragged about him, he was good in my book. As long as he continued to put a smile on her face, the two of us would never bump heads. Leilani deserved to be happy after all the bullshit she'd been through in her previous relationships. If no one else was, I was rooting for her to get her fairytale ending. With the right person by your side, they did indeed exist.

One thing I loved about my friend was that she didn't stick around to tolerate any disrespect. With Leilani, if a nigga made one wrong move, it was on to the next. Niggas like Tay got that shit confused with her being a hoe, but I saw it as her knowing what she wanted and not settling for some shit she knew wasn't going to last. I could have probably taken some notes from her in that department. I'd been with the same nigga for years, and the last few of those years, I'd been faking and pretending to be happy.

To the outside world, Tay and I had the perfect relationship, but behind closed doors, we bickered back and forth like cats and dogs. Shit, our grass could have been just as green as the other shit he compared ours to if he'd taken the time to water it. I was content with knowing that if the relationship were to end, none of it would be because of anything I'd done. All the bullshit fell solely on Tay, and when the foundation crumbled, the only person he would be able to blame was the man in the mirror. He'd singlehandedly ruined something that was supposed to be so good, and, in the end, he would have to deal with it.

"What's up, Amor?" Elijah greeted.

"Nothing much. Ready for this vacation. It's much needed. Thanks again for everything," I responded.

"It's all good, sis. Anything for my baby. Leilani can have the world if she wants it."

"Aww, that's so sweet. I love that for my friend," I said and looked over at Leilani as she beamed.

"Yeah, girl, I told Elijah he needs to set you up with one of his friends or his brother or something," Leilani interrupted.

"Oh, no, ma'am. Elijah, you can abort that mission. I'm sick of the nigga I'm with now, and I'm damn sure not in the business of recruiting anymore."

"My niggas are not clowns like that, Amor. So, when you're ready, just give me the green light," Elijah said.

Elijah was on square ball status, and if his homies or brothers were anything like him, I had to pass. I didn't know why, but I liked me a thug ass nigga; one who had some authority about him. When Tay walked into a room full of niggas, they straightened all the way up. They knew not to fuck with him, and that type of shit turned me on. Elijah wasn't Leilani's usual type, which is exactly why she ran over his ass the way she did. When he said she could have the world if she wanted it, he meant just that. Maybe that was my problem. I was chasing chocolate-covered lies when I needed to sample some caramel, or the opposite race, for that matter. My type damn sure wasn't working for me. Maybe it was time for me to stop being so closed-minded and try something new.

Once Elijah finished loading our bags into his car, we stopped to grab some food before heading to the airport. I was nervous as fuck. I'd never been on a plane before and didn't know how I managed to let Leilani talk me into getting on one. I just knew I was about to shit on myself. Leilani and Elijah both assured me that I would be fine once the plane took off and I was in the air. All I could think about was something happening and the plane going down. I'd watched too many movies and seen the craziest shit happen.

I watched from the entrance of the airport as Leilani and Elijah said their goodbyes to each other. I remembered when Tay and I were mushy and showed public affection like they were doing. So much had changed. It saddened me, but somehow, we'd lost our way, and now we'd never get back to it. I was certain we wouldn't. Apologies just couldn't change certain things, and time wasn't on Tay's side, not with me, anyway. Now that shit was being revealed to me, I had to stop making excuses for his behavior and be more realistic.

I tried to get myself together so I could find a way to board the plane. Leilani just didn't know it yet, but she would be holding my hand the entire flight.

Thankfully, there wasn't a long wait at the airport. Our fight was scheduled to leave at 1:30 that afternoon, and by 1:15, we'd put away our luggage and boarded the plane. We took our seats, and for the life of me, I didn't know why I chose to sit by the window. Everything was cool until the damn plane took off. The feeling that came over me as the engine went from a gentle purr to a giant ass roar was unlike anything I had ever experienced. Temporarily, I couldn't breathe, but after a few minutes, I was fine again. I had enough books to keep me entertained during the flight.

One of my favorite urban authors, Celeste Moore, had recently dropped a book, and I was about to get all into it. The book was titled *Who Wants That Perfect Love Anyway?* Because all her other books were so good, I knew not to expect anything less from that one. Reading was my escape from the world. Only a few people knew about my love for reading. The whole four hour and thirty-minute flight consisted of me reading and sleeping. I'd never been so ready to get to my destination in my life.

"Wake up, sleepyhead. We're here," Leilani announced as she tapped me on my shoulder.

"Dang, I guess that wasn't so bad after all."

"Yeah, you should be very well rested. I had to listen to you snore like a bear the entire flight," Leilani whined.

"Bitch, please, I do not snore," I lied.

"Amor, please. I'm pretty sure no one on the plane got any sleep because of you," she joked.

"Whatever, bitch. I was scared, and that shit fucked with my anxiety. I just may be driving back," I told her.

"Girl, please, your ass is getting right back on a plane. Besides, that's a long ass drive, and you're scared to drive on interstates, anyway."

"I guess I'm fucked, huh?" I playfully asked.

"Yes, ma'am, good and fucked. But, seriously, let's enjoy this weekend. I know it's my birthday and everything, but I'm more concerned with you letting your hair down and enjoying being away from home for a change. Whatever is going on between you and Tay, let it be until this trip is over.

"I'm good, girl, I told you. You have my word on that. I'm ready to enjoy myself and get some drinks in my system."

"Okay, well, the suite is already booked. We're staying at the Four Seasons hotel. Once we get our luggage, I guess I'll call us an Uber. If you want, we can rent a car in the morning, but I really have no plans to drive while I'm here."

"That's fine with me, and you know damn well I'm not driving, so that's dead," I informed him.

We had the hardest time locating our belongings, which was one of the biggest issues I had with flying. I'd heard of luggage and personal belongings disappearing, and I didn't have time for that shit. I was about to turn that fucking airport upside down until a nice, older white lady approached us and said they'd found our bags. I looked over at Leilani and saw her breathe a sigh of relief. I always embarrassed her when we went somewhere, but hell, that was on her. She already knew she couldn't take my ghetto ass anywhere. I never started anything, but I would damn sure finish it if I had to.

Approximately thirty minutes later, our Uber driver arrived. I couldn't help but admire him as he got out of the car and walked over to get our belongings. He was fine as fuck. He looked like he was Puerto Rican and black. He had the prettiest hazel eyes I'd ever seen, and his smile caused my heart to melt. Of course, I wouldn't have been caught dead entertaining him because I had a certain type, and he wasn't it, but it didn't hurt to look at him. After a few minutes in the car, I found out his name was Julian.

I was in awe as we pulled up to the hotel. The view was breathtaking, or maybe I just needed to get out of the house more. Whatever the case, it was beautiful.

Normally, when we'd go out somewhere, we shared a room, but Elijah had taken it upon himself to get us a two-bedroom suite. I was cool with that because I wasn't trying to hear Leilani complain about any of my habits. See, we were complete opposites, so most of the things I did easily got under her skin and vice versa. We both took about an hour to regroup and get prepared for the shenanigans that were about to come.

Good thing for me, Leilani wasn't much of a drinker because I didn't plan to turn down any drinks. If they were offered to me, I wanted them. Someone had to be the responsible one, especially since we were in a new location and didn't know anyone around. I didn't put shit past anyone. Even people we knew could have ill intentions. These days, one could never be too sure, so I learned to always expect the unexpected.

I didn't know what the hell to put on. The weather was very pleasant, and I knew I wanted to show some skin. After emptying out the contents of my suitcase, I finally decided to go with the sexy black spaghetti-strapped bodycon dress I ordered from Shein. It didn't matter how much money I had; Shein and Fashion Nova would forever get my coins. I wasn't one of those designer crazed chicks. The only time I got something designer was when it was gifted to me. I was a simple chick, and none of that shit mattered to me, which was a concept I spent most of my days trying to get that man of mine to grasp. All the money in the world wouldn't be enough to buy me. I was there because my heart was with him, and I wanted to be there; nothing more, nothing less.

I decided to wear a pair of silver heels that I also grabbed off Shein. Since the black dress had silver cutouts in the breast and hip area, they hit perfectly. I didn't feel like doing anything extravagant with my hair, so I pulled it up into a messy high bun. I left a string of hair hanging on each side of my face and wand-curled it. Makeup wasn't really my thing, but since I was out of town, I decided to go all out. Besides, it wasn't every day that my ass was in California. I owed it to myself to make the best of the experience. Whatever was going on with Tay and me could be temporarily put to the side. If the situation was reversed, that nigga wouldn't have missed out on sleep or fun, so there was no reason for me to either. Life would go on regardless.

Once I was done putting on my lashes and doing my brows, I applied a coat of lip gloss and glanced at myself one more time in the hotel bathroom's gigantic mirror. For the first time in a long damn time, I was in love with the beautiful woman I saw staring back at me. All the issues between Tay and me had me looking at myself differently, and it had done a number on my self-esteem. Being pretty was one thing, but not feeling pretty made that shit not even matter. I sprayed on some Chanel COCO perfume on my way out of my room. Then I sat on the sofa in the living room area until Leilani was done getting dressed.

I knew I would be in for a long wait, but after dealing with her for so many years, I was used to it. Leilani never being on time for anything didn't even bother me anymore. For the first time since I'd been there, I pulled my phone out of my purse and saw that I had a few messages from Tay. I cleared them without even reading them and powered my phone off. There was no way I would be able to focus on enjoying the trip if Tay was constantly trying to contact me. It screamed out that he was guilty, and I wanted that same guilt to eat his ass up.

I didn't plan to do anything more than enjoy myself with my girl while I was away, but there was no telling what thoughts would go through his head since I wasn't responding. I'd had many nights of uncertainty, and maybe he needed to feel that same shit. Maybe a dose of his own medicine would give him the act right he so desperately needed.

Leilani walked into the room and cleared her throat, redirecting my attention from my thoughts of Tay and me to her.

Coincidentally, she had on the exact same dress as I did, except her dress was silver, and the cutouts on her dress were circled in black sparkles. She had on a pair of silver and black heels. Leilani was bad as fuck too, and the dress complemented her slim-thick body perfectly.

"Not you trying to look like me!" I teased.

"Girl, please. If anything, you're trying to look like me. This dress has been sitting in my closet, collecting dust for a year and some change."

"Lei, we look bad as fuck tonight. We're about to turn all kinds of heads in the city."

"That's the plan. We're going to get you some action tonight too. Hell, I'm not saying to go fuck on no random nigga, but at least be open to the idea of meeting someone new and enjoying the vibes," Leilani expressed.

"Mmm hmm, and what about you? What are you hoping to do?" I quizzed.

"Bitch, all I got is conversation for these niggas. I'm not coming off no coochie. I don't have any coochie for no nigga, anyway. Elijah ate it all last night," she continued.

"You're so damn nasty, Lei. But I feel it."

Julian, the Uber driver from earlier that day, had given us his personal number and told us to hit him up when we were ready to get out. He said he'd drive us around at no charge, but of course, we planned to tip him generously. We didn't know him personally, but after he told us his whole life story, it was like I'd known him my whole life. I'd rather it be him who drove us around as opposed to a weirdo who gave off bad vibes. Julian didn't know which one of us to look at as he stepped out of the car to open the door for us. He was such a gentleman, and I adored that about him.

"You ladies look beautiful as hell tonight," he complimented us both.

"Thank you, Julian," we responded in unison.

I kept it very brief with him. A blind person could see that he was checking for me, and I didn't want to give him any false hope. He was easy on the eyes, and that was a fact, but I wasn't interested in him. Leilani, on the other hand, watched him from the time we got in the car to the time we got out. I made a mental note to bring that shit up later. We didn't know where we were going; we just asked Julian to take us to the most popular club San Francisco had to offer. We ended up at a spot called Temple Nightclub. That was our kind of club, and clearly, it was where people of our color partied, which was good because, personally, I hated to feel out of place.

All eyes were on Leilani and me as we strutted our way through the packed-out establishment. The niggas were drooling, and their bitches gave us the death stare. I silently prayed I wouldn't have to whoop any ass on this trip. If a bitch had the audacity to try me, I'd have to whoop her ass exactly where she had me fucked up. I wasn't checking for no other bitch's nigga, anyway. I knew firsthand the damage that could do to a woman, and I wanted no parts of it. That was the last thing a woman had to worry about where I was concerned.

I wasn't one of those bitches. Never had been, and I never would be. The thought of it disgusted me, and I honestly couldn't see how any woman was comfortable being a nigga's side piece. As women, we needed to do better by each other. A bitch was quick to holler how she didn't owe the other woman any loyalty, and that nigga did. Of course, I agreed, but that way of thinking allowed men to get away with entirely too much bullshit. I refused to be the one who helped a nigga bring misery and heartache to the next woman. I was way too real to fall victim to some shit like that.

Finally, we made our way to the bar. We were the only two females standing there and were surrounded by fine niggas.

There was a vast selection of chocolate, and it happened to come in many shapes and sizes. I was like a kid in a candy store, and Tay's trifling ass hadn't crossed my mind since we'd been at the club. I conversed with a few of the guys but nothing too major.

The last nigga who approached me had me irritated as hell. I could have been wrong, but that nigga's breath smelled like he'd just gotten back from eating somebody's ass. All I wanted at that moment was that nigga out of my fuckin' face. I could barely breathe from holding my breath for so long, and the nigga had the nerve to ramble on and on. Leilani must have noticed my facial expression because she reached for my hand and pulled me to the dance floor.

The DJ was jamming, and we showed off our best dance moves to Chris Brown's latest song, "Under the Influence." After that song went off, he played "Overdose" by Finesse2-Tymes. Everyone ran to the dance floor. There was something about that song that hyped a person up and made them want to rap the whole song word for word. After a few more songs, we made our way back to our spot at the bar. I was relieved that Mr. Shitty Breath was gone. It should have been illegal for a nigga's breath to smell that bad. Whoever the nigga was, he clearly had no friends.

Before I knew it, I was on my third Strawberry Hennessey, and I was damn sure feeling every sip of it. The feeling was everything. I wasn't worried about a damn thing at that moment and couldn't remember the last time I felt that way. I didn't know how, but Leilani had slipped away from me. I looked around and spotted her on the dance floor with none other than Julian. All I could do was shake my head and laugh at her. I knew she had a thing for him, even though she never admitted it.

The way she was grinding all over him on the dance floor

said it all. His wood had to be stiff by the time they were done dirty dancing in the middle of the damn club. It was a good thing no one knew us because that shit would have made poor Elijah have a damn heart attack. Elijah appeared to be the last thing on her mind, and I wasn't even mad at it. It was her birthday weekend, and she deserved to live it up a little. I was sure things wouldn't go any further. One thing I knew about my friend was when she was locked in with a nigga, she was locked all the way in.

Just as I was about to order another drink, the finest man I'd ever had the pleasure of laying eyes on walked up behind me.

"Get the lady whatever she's drinking, and I'll take a glass of Hennessey on the rocks," he ordered.

"That's nice of you and all, but I can pay for my own drink," I told him.

"It's no problem, and it's not that big of a deal. I was just trying to be nice," the handsome stranger insisted.

"I appreciate you. I'm not trying to be a bitch, but I've had a long day, and I'm tired as hell from my flight here this morning," I explained.

"I understand, beautiful. Where are you from, if you don't mind me asking?"

"I'm from Texas. I came here for the weekend with my best friend to celebrate her birthday."

"What's your name? My name is Chosen."

"That's an interesting name. My name is Amor," I responded.

"You mean Amor like love?" Chosen asked the same dumb ass question that most niggas tended to ask.

"Yes. After all, I am love," I sarcastically said.

"I can see that, Amor. And let my mother tell it, when she

had me, she knew I was the chosen one, which is how my name came about."

"I guess that makes sense. I can see why she would feel that way."

"I'm from the lone star state as well. I haven't been back home in, like, three going on four years. I really don't fool with my family like that."

"Wow, what a coincidence. I'm sorry to hear about you not dealing with your people. It's sad, but I understand where you're coming from because I barely fuck with my own family. Just because we have the same blood flowing through our veins doesn't necessarily make us related. That's just how I see it anyway," I expressed.

"Well said. I feel the same way. But anyway, why are you sitting over here alone and looking like you've lost your best friend or something?" Chosen asked.

"That's a long story."

"Let's hear it. I have nothing but time on my hands tonight," Chosen responded. "As a matter of fact, hold these drinks. Let's go out on the balcony. I'm sure it's not as loud out there."

"Okay. Let me go and tell my girl where I'll be, just in case she needs me," I said before I disappeared to find Leilani.

As expected, she was in a corner, hugged up with Julian. I decided to just mind my business and not say shit about it. I told her I was headed out on the balcony to chop it up with a guy I'd met and left it at that. When I made it to the balcony, Chosen was waiting for me. He was right; there weren't many people outside, and it was much quieter than inside. He was even finer with the city lights reflecting off him.

Chosen was exactly the type of man I'd go for. He was tall with a muscular build, tatted, and his waves could make a bitch seasick. Chosen had the prettiest set of perfect white teeth I'd ever seen on the opposite sex. His eyes were light brown, and the aroma of his cologne went right to my coochie. I loved myself a man with good hygiene and an impressive cologne collection. I didn't even realize I was standing there damn near in a daze, staring at him, until he called my name, snapping me out of it.

"Do you like what you see, Amor?"

"Of course I do. I wouldn't be out here with you if I didn't."

"That's good to know. I like what I see too. You're fine as a motherfucker."

"You're quite attractive yourself, Chosen. Your mother was on to something," I teased.

"Yeah, she was, huh?"

"Definitely."

"Anyway, I haven't forgotten about why we came out here. I'm all ears."

"You sure you really want to get into all of that?" I quizzed, hoping he'd change the direction of the conversation.

"Yes, ma'am, I'm positive. You'd be surprised what talking to someone you don't know can do for you. I promise you will feel much better afterward," Chosen prodded.

"Fine. Since you don't seem to be letting up, I'll talk to you. So, I have a boyfriend that I've been with for some years now. He's a good man financially, but of course, like most men, he has a hard time keeping his dick in his pants. He's a cheater, and I know that for a fact. But, for some reason, I can't seem to walk away from him. It's like, I know I deserve better, but my heart and my mind just won't get on the same page. I don't know if that makes sense to you, but that's the only way I know to explain it," I verbalized.

"I understand perfectly. It's hard to walk out on someone you've loved and shared life with for so long. Only you know when you've had enough. Trust me, beautiful, when you've had enough, you'll be able to leave without giving it a second thought. Some people come into our lives as a lesson, and maybe that's what your guy was meant to be for you. That doesn't make dude a bad person, either. It just means he's not the man for you," Chosen advised.

"I hate the thought of starting all over and having to learn someone else. He's the only man I've ever known. When I say that, I mean he's my first everything. I just wish he would get his shit together. I don't wanna leave, but I can't stay and continue to allow the disrespect from him and the bitches he chooses to deal with. I'm better than that. I know I'm not perfect. Nobody is, but I deserve better than that, especially from his ass."

"Your feelings are very valid, ma. I pray you get what you need to help you out of that situation. If he can't see what he has in front of him, he must be a damn fool, anyway."

"You're just saying that to be saying it. You don't have to do that, Chosen."

"I'm saying it because it's the truth. I can look at you and tell that you're a special woman. Special women are hard to come by. Just by this little conversation, I can tell you're a good woman, and all you need is to be loved properly," Chosen continued.

"You're right about that. Things could be so simple, but it's people who make it hard."

"I'm not going to take up too much more of your time, beautiful. I must be getting out of here. I have an early day at work in the morning. Let's go back inside and find your friend."

"That's a good idea because I need to keep an eye on her ass anyway," I responded as I closely followed Chosen back into the club.

To my surprise, Leilani was nowhere to be found, and neither was Julian. After looking for them again, Chosen offered to give me a ride back to the hotel, and I couldn't turn him down. It was either that or be stuck in a car with another Uber driver I didn't know. I didn't know Chosen either, but for some reason, I trusted him. I knew him well enough to let him drop me off, and I didn't feel like I was in harm's way or anything. I could read people, and his energy didn't give off any bad vibes. Besides, I was ready to get back to my bed and crash. My first night in Cali had been a good one. Thanks to Chosen, it was one I would probably always remember.

We continued our conversation in the car, and I was able to get into his business a bit. Chosen was an open book and didn't mind answering any of the questions I asked him. He'd been divorced for four years and hadn't been serious with anyone since his separation from his wife. According to him, his wife was the one who stepped out and cheated on him. Chosen didn't owe me any lies, so I had no choice but to take his word for everything he said. It didn't seem farfetched. Hell, just like men, some women weren't hitting on a bucket of shit, either. Chosen appeared to be the perfect man to me, but then again, I didn't really know him. I only knew what he told me. He could have been painting a pretty picture just to get my attention, but somehow, I didn't believe that.

Neither of us was ready to leave the other, so after Chosen promised to be on good behavior, I agreed to stay in his room with him. Besides, I didn't want to be alone, and I could tell he needed companionship as well. I prayed that I wouldn't do something I regretted. Though he'd promised not to be on any slick shit, it wasn't him I was worried about. The liquor I consumed had me wanting to climb his tall ass like a tree. I wondered what had gotten into me because that person damn sure wasn't the Amor I knew.

Everything about the way this man made me feel was new to me. I'd never go to a club and leave with a random man I barely knew. And I damn sure wouldn't have gotten in his car and allowed him to bypass the hotel I was staying at, only to end up at his. That was my cue to stop drinking so much. But I was there now, so I decided to just make the best of it. Besides, what was the worst that could happen?

CHAPTER SEVEN

TAY

I thanked God that Amor was gone. He had to have been looking out for me to save my dumb ass once again. As soon as Amor's car disappeared around the corner, I saw Nina's car speed up and park directly in front of the house. It was clear to me that she was on her bullshit again and looking for trouble. She was lucky that Amor was already gone, or that smile she wore would have been wiped off permanently.

I kept trying to warn her that Amor wasn't the one to play with, but she wouldn't be satisfied until she figured it out the hard way. Obviously, she wanted her face and Amor's fist to get acquainted, and I knew the day would come when I wouldn't be there to save her. When you went around looking for trouble, you would eventually find it, and Nina was damn sure looking for trouble.

"Nina, what the fuck are you doing at my house? Didn't I tell you not to ever come where my girl and I lay our heads? How the fuck do you even know where I live, anyway? Let me find out you on some stalking shit with your crazy ass."

"Well, you stopped answering my calls and texts, and I

figured that meant you wanted to talk to me in person, so here I am. You see how that works, Dontavious?"

"Nina, please, just go home. I don't have time to deal with this crazy shit you're on today."

"Nigga, I told you I was pregnant with your baby, and your response was to cut me off. Make that shit make sense."

"Let's get something straight, Nina. I cut your ass off because of that stunt you pulled. It had nothing to do with you being pregnant. For all I know, you could be lying about being pregnant, and even if you are, that doesn't mean it's mine. I know I'm not the only nigga smashing you, so you can miss me with all that."

"Well, aren't you the typical nigga? Were you thinking about any of that bullshit you just said when you were running up in me raw? If it's one thing I don't play about, it's my fuckin kids, Dontavious. Please don't make me take it there with you," Nina threatened.

"Bitch, is that a threat?"

"Naw, nigga, that's a fuckin' promise. I understand you're trying to protect your relationship, but you're not going to come at me like I'm just some kind of hoe or something. This baby I'm carrying is your child, whether you like it or not. Either you're going to step up to the plate and be a man, or I'll be forced to handle the situation how I see fit," Nina informed me, and I could tell by her tone that she wasn't playing any games with my ass.

"Nina, calm down. You're getting yourself all worked up over nothing. All I'm saying is, I want to be a hundred percent sure that baby belongs to me. I have a lot on the line to lose, man, and you know that shit."

"Once again, nigga, were you thinking about what you had to lose when you were raw dogging me and asking if you could nut in this good pussy?" Nina interrogated as she rolled those pretty brown eyes of hers.

"Hell naw, I wasn't. Now stop asking me those dumb ass questions. You know none of that shit crossed my mind in the heat of the moment. But if memory serves me correctly, your lying ass said you couldn't get pregnant because you were on birth control," I recalled.

"Nigga, none of that shit is a hundred percent accurate. I guess this shit was just meant to be. Either way it goes, Dontavious, we're here now."

"Yeah, but we don't have to be, Nina."

"Dontavious, what the fuck are you hinting at? Nigga, I know you're not insinuating that I get rid of my child, so you can get a free pass from the choices you made. Please tell me that's not what you're saying to me."

"Nina, stop with all the sentimental shit because you know damn well you don't need another child right now. You can barely deal with lil' Jay without getting bent out of shape. The only reason you want this child is to have something to hold over a nigga's head."

"Please don't flatter yourself, Dontavious. I don't rock with that abortion bullshit. So, you can get that shit out of your head."

"Okay, Nina, but you having my child won't change our situation. I still do not want to be with you. Even if Amor decided to leave my black ass, I will never be with you," I spat, irritated by her antics.

"That's cool too. Just know that I'm going to make your life a living hell. Tread lightly, Dontavious. Tread the fuck lightly. I'm warning you not to get on my bad side. Because, once you do, you have to stay there forever," Nina said as she got into her car and dramatically drove off.

I could smell the scent of her tires burning. I'd never

regretted dealing with Nina on that level until that very moment. By that time, all the neighbors had gathered around and were talking amongst themselves. We were one of three black couples on the entire block, so I guess they were shocked to get that kind of entertainment. I hoped and prayed none of the women mentioned it to Amor. She'd become a hot commodity in the neighborhood, and all the women flocked to her. My girl didn't have a problem fitting in with anyone, and everyone loved her.

Maybe I was wrong for suggesting that Nina get an abortion. Hell, maybe I was even wrong for implying that she was sexually involved with other niggas besides me. That was her pussy, though, and I had no idea if she was giving that snapper to someone else or not. I didn't feel like it was right for her to be so mad about my wanting to be sure before I jumped into anything headfirst. I'd been in the same situation twice before, and both times the child ended up not being mine. The only difference was I didn't have the problems I had from Nina with either of those women.

If I made one wrong move, Nina was there waiting, so she could fuck my life up. Nina wanted to be in Amor's shoes so bad, but little did she know, those were some big shoes to fill, and her ass couldn't walk a mile in them.

I was pissed at Nina but madder at myself than anything because I should have known better than to do some shit to land me in that situation. The shit was crazy. I had the girl who everyone wanted. One who didn't want anything from me but me, not someone whose loyalty or intentions I had to question, and I still found a way to fuck that up. I wasn't only referencing the shit with Nina, but everything I did. I was dead ass wrong, and I owned that shit.

As a man, I knew what I had to do. I knew what I had to say to Amor would break her beautiful heart, but with the way

Nina was carrying on, it was too much of a risk not to go ahead and tell her myself. If she were to hear the shit from someone else's mouth, a possible reconciliation would be out of the question. For some reason, I hadn't lost all hope just yet. Real love was said to conquer all, and if nothing else, our love was real.

Amor was on her trying to get under my skin shit because she hadn't so much as picked up the phone and called to let me know she'd landed safely. Had it not been for the pictures of her and Leilani's thot ass with the location on, I wouldn't have known a damn thing. I texted her a few times, only to not get an answer. When I called her, and it went straight to her voice-mail, I knew she'd turned her phone off. Hardly ever did she just allow her phone to die.

Amor was pissed at me and needed her space, and I didn't blame her for it. I wanted her to have a good time and possibly get her mind off all the negative things. I trusted her not to do anything she didn't have any business doing. Amor was a woman in a relationship, and she knew how to carry herself in that manner. I'd never been given a reason to think otherwise, so I wasn't going to start today. If time was what she needed, time was what I would give her. I couldn't do shit but respect her wishes. Pressuring her would only make her want to stray further away from me, and that was the last thing I needed.

With everything I had going on in my personal life, I had started to neglect what I had going on business-wise. So much shit was going on in the streets, and it was up to me to get shit back in order. Niggas were straight wilding, and they were only doing the shit because they knew I wasn't there to see it. All I had to do was simply show my face for all those niggas to fall in line. I was a playful ass nigga who laughed and joked about plenty of shit, but my money and my respect were not among those things.

CHAPTER EIGHT

AMOR

The sun shining through the window caused me to wake up bright and early. I was still wrapped in Chosen's arms, and the shit gave me butterflies. I couldn't recall the last time something felt so good. The intimacy between Chosen and me was even better than sex. The fact that he was able to lay there all night and hold me while I wore nothing but one of his t-shirts and my panties underneath told me a lot about his character.

Chosen was a real man and wasn't on the little boy bullshit. His mindset was just as attractive as he was, and I loved everything about him. I wished I could stay cuddled in bed with him for the rest of the morning, but I knew Leilani would have a fuckin' fit if I didn't get back to the hotel to help her get her day started. It wasn't every day that a woman turned twenty-three.

Chosen was sleeping so peacefully that I almost hated to wake him up. Somehow, I managed to slip out of the tight grip he had on me and went into the bathroom to wash my face and

.ush my teeth. I was glad he had an extra toothbrush there because I wouldn't have said a word to him the whole ride back to my room. I contemplated just calling an Uber so I wouldn't have to wake him at all, but by the time I was done in the bathroom, he was already awake.

"Good morning, sleepyhead."

"Good morning, beautiful. I don't know how I got any sleep because you snore like a grown ass man."

"That means I was comfortable next to you."

"Oh, that's what it means, huh?"

"Yes, indeed. Besides, I told you I was tired from the flight, and all those drinks I took down last night didn't help any."

"I can believe it, ma. You slept like a newborn baby last night."

"I feel rejuvenated and ready to take on the day. Today is my bestie's birthday, and I'm sure she has all kinds of shit planned for us to do," I shared.

"That's what's up, ma. Y'all enjoy yourselves. There are a lot of things to do around here, so you won't be bored unless you want to be."

"Okay, well, whenever you get situated, you can drop me off. I'm not in any rush, so take your time."

"Okay. Let me hop in the shower, and once I get dressed, I'll drop you off. I have to pass that hotel to get to my job, anyway."

While I waited for Chosen to get ready, I powered my phone on and texted Leilani to let her know I'd be there soon. When I turned it on, all kinds of messages from Tay came through, and one from Leilani, letting me know she'd left the club with Julian. I decided to text Tay and let him know I was fine, so he didn't have to worry about me. Little did he know, I was in real good hands.

I damn near choked on the coffee I was sipping when

Chosen walked out of the bathroom with his dick swinging like it was happy to see me. I mean, that motherfucker was bouncing with joy. In awe, I watched the water drip from his body. I damn near wanted to get on my knees and talk into his mic, but I talked myself out of it. Chosen had gotten way too comfortable around me, but then again, I was in his personal space. I enjoyed the view as I watched him get dressed like a damn pervert or something.

Though he wasn't shy and clearly wanted me to see what he had to offer, it felt like I was doing something wrong. Whew, that man was a different breed of fine. Luckily, he was pressed for time because of the meeting he had at work, and I had to get back to the room to get my day started. Once he was dressed and sprayed some cologne that smelled like the name of it could have been, *Come Fuck Me,* we headed to the car. When we pulled up to the hotel where I was staying, he asked me the question I'd been dreading.

"Can I see you again tonight? I mean, if it's possible," Chosen asked.

"Once I figure out what's on the itinerary for today, I'll let you know. If so, it'll be much later," I responded.

"That's fine, baby. Some of the fellas and I are going out tonight too. So, maybe we can just link up afterward. Here, just put my number in your phone. Maybe you'll stay with me again tonight," he expressed.

"You would like that, wouldn't you?" I playfully asked. Hell, I would like that too.

"I would love that. I kept my word and was a perfect gentleman, right?"

"I can't argue with you there because you absolutely were. I don't know if I could have been that strong if I were you, and all this ass was pressed against me," I joked.

"Yeah, I did wake up with a boner while you sitting your

pretty ass over there joking. It's all good, though. I enjoyed your company."

"So did I, but what I enjoyed most was going to sleep and waking up still in your arms," I admitted.

"That was nice, huh, Amor?"

"It really was. Let me go, but I'll be in touch. Have a great day at work, Chosen."

"You have a good day as well. And tell your friend I said Happy Birthday. Maybe you can introduce us later."

"Hopefully so."

As I stepped out of Chosen's car, the first thing that caught my attention was a car that looked like Julian's. I had to be mistaken; there were probably a hundred cars like his in the city. I knew Leilani wasn't doing it like that, not with how she claimed to be so in tune with Elijah. When I walked into the room, all my suspicions were confirmed. I came face to face with Julian as he was about to leave the room. I just looked at him, speechless and coming up short when I tried to find the words to say.

I sat on the edge of Leilani's bed and waited for her to get out of the shower. She stepped out singing love songs and shit and was shocked when she saw me sitting there. Leilani rolled her eyes before she fixed her mouth to say anything to me.

"Nothing happened, Amor, so please stop looking at me like that. Worry about what you were doing that you didn't come back to the room at all last night," she snapped.

"Fair enough, girl, but for the record, Chosen and I didn't do anything either. That man held me in his arms all night, and I needed that affection. Not to mention he allowed me to vent and get all my feelings out about what's going on in my relationship."

"Whoever this Chosen person is, he sounds like exactly

what the doctor ordered. I already like him more than I have ever liked Tay's goofy ass."

"I figured you would feel that way, Lei. He's pretty damn amazing." I beamed.

"I bet he is. Go ahead and get ready. I have a full day planned for us," Leilani said.

"I figured you would. What's the dress code?"

"Chill. We're not going anywhere but shopping and on a boat ride right now. Save your thot fits for later tonight," she joked.

We hit a few stores and ran up a bag at Tay and Elijah's expense. The stores there had way more to offer than the ones back in Texas. Everything that caught my eye, I got that shit. After all, Tay told me to get whatever I wanted, and that money wasn't an issue. Who was I not to follow directions? That nigga wasn't wanting for shit and could get every dime I spent back by the end of the next day. I even managed to sneak and get Leilani a birthday gift when she wasn't paying attention.

I owed her for how our girl's trip had turned out so far. It had exceeded my expectations from day one, and I couldn't seem to get Chosen off my mind. Everything about that man was so damn addictive. Normally, I wouldn't have been so quick to brag on a nigga, but something was so different about him. I didn't know where things between the two of us were even headed, considering the mess of a situation I had at home. Some heavy soul-searching and thinking needed to be done on my end.

I tried not to act off emotion because I knew it would cost me every time. The last thing I wanted to do was make a wrong decision and end up in an even worse situation than the one I was already in. But, on the other hand, whether I chose to pursue a relationship with Chosen or not, I still needed to get away from Tay. That not being appreciated or loved properly shit was over and done with.

After we did everything Leilani had planned for us that day, we went back to the room and got dressed, so we could find another club to hit. Although I was enjoying myself, I couldn't wait to see Chosen again. We'd been texting for the majority of the day, and he'd given me a club recommendation. It was the same club where he and his friends would be. It took some convincing, but finally, I convinced Leilani to go to the Lush Lounge instead of the club she originally planned for us to hit. It was her weekend, and we were supposed to do what she wanted, but I had to see Chosen. I knew she would understand. After all, she was the one who wanted me to get over Tay and under someone new.

Once again, Shein won as my outfit of choice for the night. After taking a shower and moisturizing my body all over, I slipped into a red jumpsuit. My feet were still killing me from the night before, so I decided to play it safe and slipped on some cute clear sandals. I let my hair down from the messy bun and styled it. I wanted to look good for Chosen. He'd mentioned that red was his favorite color, and he liked his women natural without all the extra shit. So, besides my eyebrows, I went bare-faced.

The vibe in the Lush Lounge was just about the same as the first club we'd gone to. I even remembered seeing some of the same people from the night before. The spot was packed out, and there were some fine niggas in the building. None of them were fine enough to take my mind off the person it was on, though. I looked around the club in search of Chosen, but he was nowhere to be found. Finally, I pulled my phone out and glanced at our messages again to make sure I had the right spot.

Leilani was already at the bar and had ordered our drinks when I got there. She was all in her phone, and I already knew Julian had her attention. I assumed it wouldn't be long before he showed up somewhere. I tried my hardest to enjoy myself, but I couldn't even lie; I was in a funk until someone tapped me on my shoulder. I turned around, ready to slap a nigga for having the nerve to touch me, but when I realized it was Chosen, my whole face lit up. I couldn't have hidden my excitement if I tried. He had me gone, and the crazy thing about it was he knew it. From the way he was cheesing and showing all his teeth, I wanted to believe the feeling was mutual.

"Sorry I'm late, beautiful. Work ran a little over, and the guys hit another spot before coming here," Chosen informed me.

"It's all good. I knew you would show your face before the night was over. We were going to have a problem had you stood me up," I joked.

"You want something else to drink? Birthday girl, can I get you anything?" Chosen asked.

"I'll take a Sex on the Beach," I responded.

"Yes, I'll take one of those as well. Thank you," Leilani expressed.

"It's all good, ma."

"Let me get a proper introduction going on. Chosen, this is my best friend, Leilani. Leilani, this is—" I couldn't even finish my sentence before he cut me short.

"I'm Chosen, her future man," he continued.

"I heard that shit, and trust me when I say I'm here for all of that," Leilani responded.

"Let's not get too far ahead of ourselves," I added, trying to be hard.

How that nigga had me feeling, he just didn't know. He

could be anything he wanted to be. Chosen referring to himself as my future man made me feel every bit of crazy. I wasn't even mad at it, though. I could see him being my man and so much more. Meeting him at a time when everything was so crazy in my life was strange, but it was like God gave me what I needed exactly when I needed it. I wanted to believe Tay was the one for me, but a man who hurt me as much as he did couldn't really love me. I was being punished. I wouldn't leave him of my own free will, so God allowed him to hurt me so many times until I would just get tired and cut my losses.

When I really thought about it, I was a damn fool for staying and putting up with his shit for as long as I did. Had it been anyone else, I would have talked about them like a dog, but since it was me being dumb, I swept the shit under the rug.

My biggest fear was explaining my hurt to Chosen, only for him to turn around and do the same foul shit to me. I didn't expect him to be perfect because I knew perfect people didn't exist, but I just wanted to get it right with someone who had the same genuine intentions that I did. I craved real love minus the bullshit and game-playing. Chosen didn't give me any bad vibes, nor had he displayed any fuck boy traits, but then again, I'd only known him for a minute. In the beginning, it was always lies and butterflies, and everything was always too good to be true.

After we'd all had way too many drinks, I was ready to go. Leilani and Julian were off in a corner by themselves boo'd up while I sat at one of the tables with Chosen and his homies. Some other bitches made their way to our table and threw themselves at his boys. I wished a bitch would have tried to come at Chosen the wrong way while I was sitting right there beside him. I peeped them looking and lusting after him, but while I was in the city, he belonged to me.

Chosen never even looked up at them, and that gave him

some brownie points in my book. Had it been Tay, the nigga would have been drooling from the damn mouth and wouldn't have cared if I noticed him looking at the women or not.

In a room full of badass attractive women, Chosen only had eyes for me. That was the kind of shit a chick like me could get used to. I whispered in his ear and told him I was ready to leave. We excused ourselves, and one of his drivers was waiting when we stepped outside. The man greeted him with such respect. I'd never been chauffeured around before, so it was a new experience for me. To my surprise, we bypassed all the hotels, and about forty minutes later, we pulled up to a big ass gate where Chosen had to enter a password to get in.

I was in awe as we drove past all the big ass mansions in the gated community. It was something that I had only seen before in movies I'd watched on television. When we finally stopped, the first thing I noticed was the cars parked in the driveway. The cars consisted of a Rolls-Royce, Range Rover, and a Mercedes-Maybach S-Class. All of them were black and shining. I could look at Chosen and easily tell he had money, but never in a million years did I imagine he lived like this.

Once his driver came around and opened the door, we got out. I followed Chosen like a puppy seeing its new home for the first time. I tried to hold back my excitement, but I knew my face told exactly what I didn't want to say.

"Wow, Chosen. This is beautiful. The view is breathtaking," I finally found the words to say.

"Thanks, beautiful. This is just one of the many homes I own. I have another spot on the other side of town. I also have one in Texas, along with a few rental properties," he responded.

"Dang, so does that make you a millionaire or something?" I quizzed.

"No, ma'am, that makes me a billionaire. At first, I was

going to wait to bring you here, but since I'm really feeling you, I just thought you should know everything about me."

"I understand. So, what exactly do you do for a living?" I inquired.

"I went to school and studied real estate. After working for my family's company for so many years, I decided to branch off and start my own. That, along with good investments in stocks and mutual funds, set me up for life. My money literally makes me more money. The goal for me was always to be financially free, if you know what I mean," Chosen explained.

"That's amazing. I'm glad everything worked out in your favor."

"Baby, I'm thirty-two years old. I couldn't see myself punching the clock forever. I wanted better, so I had to train my mind to believe I could do better. We can be anything we want to be. Remember that."

"Can I have a tour of the house?"

"Of course, you can. Hopefully, you'll be living here with me soon," Chosen responded with a smirk.

The tour of the house ended in his bedroom. His bedroom was the size of my whole damn house, not to mention the huge walk-in closets. I could see all my clothes and shoes occupying the shelves. When I sat on the bed, I sank into it like it was about to swallow me. I'd never been in a bed so comfortable.

Chosen walked over to the dresser and pulled out one of his white Polo t-shirts for me to sleep in. I stood up long enough to get undressed and slip the shirt on. I didn't even care that he was watching me get undressed. After the way he'd taunted me that morning with his little strip tease, he had it coming.

He walked up behind me and gently kissed me on the back of my neck while he rubbed my shoulders. My body welcomed his touch, and my pussy started to purr. Chosen turned me around, so I was facing him, lifted my chin, and kissed me in a way that I had never been kissed before. Our tongues danced as his hands continued to explore my body. I giggled a little as they cupped my ass cheeks, and he playfully smacked it. I gently bit my lip as his fingers found my opening and started to massage my clit.

"Mhhhm," I moaned, never breaking our stare.

I watched him as he removed his fingers and placed them in his mouth. Seeing him taste my sweet pussy juices had me ready for him to bury his face between my legs.

"You taste so good, Amor," he stopped long enough to compliment.

As if he'd read my mind, he picked me up, placed me on his shoulders, and started going to work on my pussy. Each flick of his tongue on my clit made me cry out even louder. Chosen was no amateur in the pussy eating department. He took his time and devoured me. It was crazy how he knew all my spots and exactly what to do to get me there. My body started to shake uncontrollably, letting us both know that an orgasm was near. As if he really wanted to make me go crazy, he inserted two fingers and continued to please me with his tongue. I came repeatedly and didn't want it to end.

When Chosen finally let me down, my legs felt like spaghetti, and I could barely stand long enough to walk to the bed. That was the true definition of being weak in the knees. I watched quietly as Chosen started to undress. When he freed his dick from his boxers, it bounced up and down like it was on hydraulics. That thang was thangin' as the girls would say, and he had the prettiest penis I'd ever seen.

He walked over and got in bed beside me. "Come here."

I climbed on top of him and gently eased his thick, long

dick inside me, inch by inch. It took me a few minutes to adjust to his girth, but once I was, I started bouncing up and down on it. Every so often, I would bring down my speed and slow grind on his dick while looking him dead in his eyes. The sound of him moaning and saying some other shit turned me on so bad. I didn't know what it was, but something about hearing a man moan did it for me.

"Oh, my God, CHOSEN! It feels so good!" I screamed as I continued to bounce up and down on his dick.

"That's right, beautiful. Ride daddy's dick, just like that."

It wasn't until we ended up in the missionary position that I realized I'd bitten off way more than I could chew. All I could do was wrap my legs around Chosen as he thrusted deep inside me. It was the kind of hurt that felt so damn good. For the first time, I cried actual tears as I worked my hips underneath him. The eye contact, intensity, and mood were unmatched.

I could tell by the way Chosen was fuckin' me that he was about to nut. Why I didn't push his ass off me or ask him to pull out, I didn't know, but instead, he released his semen right inside me. If I didn't know any better, I would've thought he made love to me, but we didn't love each other, so I chalked it up to us having some amazing ass sex. I lost count of how many times I orgasmed.

After we were done with our bomb ass sex session, I excused myself from the bedroom to take a shower. Once inside, I cried my eyes out. What I'd done with Chosen was my only sexual encounter with a man other than Tay. I didn't know how to feel about the shit, either. I liked Chosen and all, but I had never been the type to just go around sleeping with men I'd just met. Against my better judgment, I let my emotions get the best of me. One moment of weakness caused me to do something I would most likely regret. Tay had me tripping and acting way outside my character. I couldn't be mad at Chosen because he was only being a man, and with the way he'd put it on me, he would always be good in my book.

Before I could get out of the shower, Chosen stepped in and asked if he could join me. Who was I to tell him what he couldn't do inside his own home? Once again, he buried his head between my thighs and lapped away at my juices.

"I didn't know I was starving until I tasted you," he muttered and then went right back to what he was doing down there.

When Chosen finally came up for air, he picked me up and positioned me on his dick. I held onto the shower rod as I rode him for dear life. I wasn't sure what turned me on the most—the way he sucked on my titties or the passionate kisses he placed on my neck while he tightly wrapped both hands around it. Once he was satisfied with how many times he'd made me reach my peak, we actually showered and headed to bed. I had a flight to catch in a couple of hours.

One thing was for sure; I was leaving California even more confused than when the plane landed there. The point of the whole trip, in the first place, was to get away and find peace of mind. I needed to figure things out and think about my next steps. Now, I was back at square one. Instead of it only being Tay on my dome, Chosen had just as much space in my mind as he did. Hell, what was even worse was the fact that I didn't even want to leave Chosen behind. True, we'd only been acquainted for a short time, but he'd made me feel things the man I'd been with for years wasn't able to make me feel. He took the time to listen to me and understand me. With everything he had going on in his life, he made time for me, and that meant more to me than anything else in the world. Any nigga could blow a bag on a woman, especially when he had the money to do it, but not every nigga would give a woman their time. To me, that was the factor that set real men apart. Chosen was as real as they came, for sure.

Early the next morning, I was awakened by the aroma of bacon, grits, eggs, and waffles. When it hit my nose, it caused me to hop my ass up almost instantly. Since Chosen was rich, I figured I'd walk into the kitchen and find one of his chefs cooking. To walk in and see him standing in front of the stove throwing down instead warmed my heart a little. I wasn't used to shit like that, so I didn't know how to act. During the years I'd been with Tay, I couldn't even remember him attempting to boil me a hotdog. So, I appreciated Chosen's kind gesture.

"Good morning, sleepy head," he greeted as I took a seat at the kitchen table.

"Good morning, you. It smells so good in here. I can't believe you're in here cooking," I responded.

"Don't you think you're worth it?" Chosen asked. "Normally, I wouldn't be in here cooking, but Doris is on vacation this week. Her food probably tastes way better than mine, but I do just fine."

"I'm sure you do too. A man has never cooked for me before, so I'm excited and ready to dig in."

"Never? Amor, you've been missing out on some things. I hate to judge, but it's sad, honestly."

"It's okay. I couldn't agree more. I get the feeling all of that is about to change soon."

"It sure is... If you want it to, that is. The ball is in your court, Amor. I've laid my cards out there," Chosen reminded me.

"I know you have, but it's not as simple as you're making it sound. I have some things to figure out at home first. I can't just jump headfirst into something else before I've handled the situation I'm already in," I tried to explain, but Chosen wasn't trying to hear that excuse.

"You know it's not as complicated as you're making it either, beautiful. That nigga doesn't appreciate you, and things taken for granted eventually get taken. Just so you know, I have no intention of letting up. I want you, Amor, and I won't rest until you're permanently in my arms," Chosen verbalized.

I cleared my throat before I spoke again because what the hell was I supposed to say behind that?

"You're absolutely right about everything you said, Chosen. That's even more of a reason for me to get back home and figure all this shit out. If I said I didn't want you as well, I would be blatantly lying because clearly, there is a deep connection between us. Just give me a little time, okay? If it's meant for us to be part of each another's lives, we will be," I expressed.

"You got it, ma. I'm not going anywhere, but don't get back home and just forget about a nigga. Keep in touch. I'll be that way soon for a family function, and I would like to see you then."

"Of course. Just keep me posted on the dates, and we can make something happen. This food is delicious, by the way. You know your way around the kitchen and some pussy, I see," I teased.

"Thank you, baby. I try to be the best in everything I do. You better go get dressed, so I can get you back to the room. I almost forgot you have a flight to catch in a few hours."

"Damn, I guess I let time get away from me," I uttered as I looked at the time on the clock.

"That's what happens when you're where you're supposed to be."

The entire car ride back to the room was silent. Chosen and I held hands, and he held me close in his arms. It was a feeling that I damn near needed and one I damn sure wasn't ready to let go of. When he touched me, it was like my body melted. The effect that man had on me was like an out-of-body experience. Maybe he was the man for me after all, and I was just too blinded by my feelings for Tay to realize it.

With the way he pressured me, I didn't have much time to make up my mind. I hated to be pressured, but I understood where Chosen was coming from. I knew it wasn't fair to ask him to wait for me, and honestly, I didn't even expect him to. The thought of someone else getting the same treatment he'd given me made me fume on the inside. Chosen was a good ass man, so I knew he wouldn't be on the market for long.

When the driver pulled up to the hotel and opened my door for me, Chosen and I said our goodbyes. He pulled me in for what seemed like the longest embrace ever. As Chosen ran his fingers through my hair, he said he enjoyed his time spent with me, and he hoped to see me soon. I wanted to fall apart right in front of him because I was so deep in my feelings. He was all the things I'd ever prayed for in a man. I wasn't the type who believed in love at first sight, but Chosen had my mind blown. Was it possible to love two men at the same time? I was slipping and needed to get myself together. I couldn't even wrap my mind around everything that had occurred over the little time I'd been in California.

When I got to the room, Leilani was packing her bags. She didn't have a lot to say, which wasn't normal behavior for her. I could tell she was happy, though. She'd enjoyed her birthday, which was all that really mattered. With the way she had carried on with Julian, I imagined she felt just as conflicted as I did. We both had received way more than we'd bargained for, and that wasn't such a bad thing after all. Being around

Chosen opened my eyes to a lot of things. Now that I had a taste of how I was supposed to be treated, I refused to settle for anything less. Tay wasn't a bad person, but he wasn't the best that he could be either. It was time for him to make some serious changes, and if he wasn't willing, that would tell me everything I needed to know.

Once we'd packed all our belongings and done a sweep of the room to ensure that we hadn't forgotten anything, we headed for the hotel lobby, where Julian was waiting to drop us off at the airport. I hopped in the back seat, and Leilani sat up front with Julian. I observed their body language and the way they couldn't keep their eyes off each other. Sparks flew, and I knew for a fact that Leilani had let Julian's fine ass clap her cheeks. I didn't want to press the issue since I knew she'd tell me when she felt the time was right.

We never kept things from each other, and I was sure we wouldn't start any time soon. I, for one, couldn't wait to tell her how Chosen had rocked my world. Hell, I didn't even know if I had any pussy left after the way he'd eaten it. I got chills just from thinking about the shit.

My reaction to being on the plane was totally different from how it was on the flight there. Even the departure didn't bother me because I had so much other shit on my mind. I wondered how I would even look Tay in the face when I got back home. The guilt from my time spent with Chosen had started to eat me alive. Knowing that I'd granted him access to my body, the main thing that I'd kept sacred for so many years, was the tip of the iceberg. If Tay were ever to find out that piece of information, my ass would probably be dead somewhere, never to be found.

Niggas were always dishing out shit that they would never be able to take. Just knowing another nigga got some of what was supposed to be his would have him ready to kill everything that moved. It was something I planned to keep to myself. Chosen would be one of my best kept secrets.

"Damn, girl, what are you over there cheesing about?" Leilani asked.

"My bad, girl. My ass over here having sex flashbacks and shit," I beamed.

"Chosen put it on you like that, huh?"

"Bitch! That man is skilled, and not to mention, extremely blessed, if you know what I mean. I've never been fucked like that before. I swear I've been missing out on life, friend. And to think, all this time, I thought Tay was really doing something," I said as I shook my head.

"Damn, girl, what did that man do to you?" Leilani quizzed.

"What didn't he do would be a better question. He did everything to me. He ate me for breakfast, lunch, and dinner too."

"Damn, I'm jealous," Leilani playfully said.

"Girl, sex with Chosen was amazing. It was so intimate, so passionate, so different from what I was used to."

"Snap out of it, bitch. You're talking like you're in love with that man or something. Remember, you're about to go home to your own nigga. So, don't get yourself caught up."

"Bitch, don't you think I know that? I'm not in love with Chosen, but I can damn sure see it getting to that point if I continue talking to him. That man treated me like a fuckin' queen from the moment we met," I explained.

"I get it. Trust me, I do. Julian and I hit off as well. We didn't have sex or anything like that, but we did get close to it. I just couldn't go through with doing it, knowing Elijah was home waiting for me and was the reason I was on the damn trip in the first place. Elijah is a damn good man, and I know he loves me, but we don't have anything in common when I really think about it. Julian gets me," Leilani expressed.

"I don't know about all of that, but he damn sure kept a smile on your face the entire weekend. You were happier these last few days than I've ever seen you with a man. That says a lot."

"I know, right? Amor, I can't even lie. I'm so confused, and I'm having all kinds of mixed emotions about the situation. I would never want to do anything to hurt Elijah because I wouldn't want him to hurt me. He doesn't deserve for his feelings to be toyed with."

"Just take some time and put yourself first. Think about what you want. You gotta do whatever to make yourself happy. Your happiness is what matters the most. Hell, if Julian the Uber driver makes you happy, I say go for it. You only get one life. Isn't that what you told me?"

"Yes, but those were different circumstances. Tay deserves exactly what he got. His feelings deserve to be played with for all the shit he's put you through. I just want you to make sure you know what you're doing. Don't make any decisions based on temporary feelings and emotions."

"You're right. I have some thinking to do as well. I don't even know if I'm going to keep in touch with Chosen or not. I told him I would, but I'm having second thoughts. Maybe it was only meant to be what it was. I needed him, and I feel like he needed me too. Us crossing paths wasn't an accident."

"You never know, Amor. Chosen could be your soulmate. If I were you, I wouldn't X him out of the picture just yet. He could be the one God has for you, and if that's the case, I hope you don't let Tay keep you away from him. Because Tay damn sure isn't the one for you," Leilani insisted.

"I've been feeling that way too, lately. I really have. Ever since that bitch called my man's phone, I've been looking at him sideways. I know there is something more to that story. I just know there is."

"You already know it is. It's going to reveal itself sooner or later. If she was bold enough to call his phone, knowing he was home with you, then she's going to pop up again. She wants you to know about her. I hate those kinds of bitches with a passion, friend," Leilani continued her rant.

CHAPTER NINE

TAY

I was on pins and needles waiting for Amor to arrive back home, especially not knowing what kind of mood she would be in. For some reason, I couldn't help but feel like shit was about to go from bad to worse. With Nina's delusional ass popping up at the house and all the neighbors seeing the shit, I knew it was only a matter of time before word got back to Amor. If people minded their business, it wouldn't have even been an issue, but that wasn't the case. Living in a white neighborhood was just as bad as being amongst our own kind.

Those bitches kept up more shit than a little bit, which was probably why they were always crying to Amor about their husbands cheating on them. It wouldn't have surprised me if Amor had already heard about what happened, though I prayed she hadn't. The last thing I wanted was to be arguing with my girl as soon as she stepped in the door. I'd missed her stubborn ass like crazy while she was gone, and I just wanted us to put our heads together and figure some shit out. I could tell she was ready to break free, but I refused to believe that it was the end for us. We'd overcome way too many obstacles together.

I went back and forth with myself, trying to decide if I wanted to go ahead and break the news to her about Nina and the maybe baby she was carrying. There was no right time to deliver that type of news, so to say I was waiting for the perfect time sounded ridiculous. Amor was a strong ass woman, and she'd remained by my side through some of the most fucked up situations. Possibly having a kid by another bitch was something I didn't think she would ever forgive me for.

I was used to her leaving to clear her head for a few days or maybe even weeks, depending on what I'd done. But the shit I'd gotten myself into seemed final like there wasn't any coming back from it. Where would I even start trying to make things right with Amor? The trust had been broken a long time ago, and how would we move forward with a baby in the picture to constantly remind her of how I messed up?

I was wrong for wanting Nina to get an abortion, and I knew it was selfish of me to even suggest it. The only thing I cared about was saving my relationship with Amor, though. I'd take the rest up with God. Besides, it wasn't like Nina even wanted the damn baby in the first place. She would only use the child as a pawn to get what she wanted from me, and that wasn't right either. I knew my woman, and she would eventually get over me cheating like she always did. But she would never forgive me for getting a bitch pregnant.

Nina had really gotten beside herself, and I hoped and prayed she wouldn't pull the stunt again that she pulled while Amor was gone. She left the house mad as fuck, and there was no telling what she would do next. Nina was delusional and unstable; I should have known better because the signs of her being batshit crazy were always there. At first, the shit she did and said was cute to me. I got a thrill out of knowing I had her head gone. The way bitches acted behind me further let me know I was that nigga. But it didn't take long for it to get old.

I'd taken it upon myself to get some nice things for Amor. I hit all her favorite spots because I just wanted to see a smile on her face again. I couldn't recall the last time I had seen her happy or without a frown on her face. Knowing I was the reason for it made me feel so fuckin' bad. Amor was the only woman who could break me down emotionally. Her feelings were the only ones I cared about. I so badly wanted to man up for her and get it right, but something told me I had waited a little too late. I could tell Amor had finally reached her breaking point and started to lose interest in me. As the saying goes, *when she stops bitching, she's not your bitch anymore.* Amor hadn't been bothering me about anything. It was like she didn't care anymore.

Finally, I heard her car pull into the driveway, so I abruptly jumped up to help her with her luggage. I didn't want her to struggle with carrying the heavy suitcases by herself. I was certain they were even heavier than before they left with all the shopping she'd done while she was away. All I could do was shake my head when I got the notifications on my phone. Amor hit a nigga so hard that the people were calling me to see if the charges were fraudulent. The phone call made me laugh because I knew Amor was only doing it to get back at me, and she was still upset about the situation that had transpired.

I didn't give a damn, though. She could have maxed that motherfucker out for all I cared. If it meant not having to hear her mouth, I was all for it. I took a deep breath before walking outside, hoping I wasn't walking into any smoke. For the first time ever, I swear I didn't want any problems with her.

"Hey, baby," I greeted. "How was the trip? Did y'all have a good time?

"Hey, babe. It was nice. We had a really good time," Amor softly responded.

"That's good. I'm glad y'all enjoyed yourselves. I'm glad you're back home. It's been too quiet around here."

"I'm so tired from that long-ass flight. I just want to take a shower and take a nap," she commented.

"Do that then, baby. You need me to run out and grab you anything?" I asked.

"Sure, some food and some snacks would be nice. I don't plan to dot that door at all for the rest of the day."

"Okay, baby, I got you. Just relax, and I'll take care of that for you."

"Thank you. I appreciate you."

"It's all good, baby. I love you."

"Love you too," Amor responded before walking into the house and leaving me to fight with her bags.

She knew I hated that *love you too* shit. To me, *love you too,* and *I love you too* had different meanings. But considering how cold she had been to me lately, I decided to leave well enough alone. I was happy she said that much. Besides her normal sarcasm, Amor was in a good mood. Once she got inside and saw all the shit I bought her, that mood would only improve.

On the way to the store, Nina called my phone five times back to back. I didn't have shit to say to her retarded ass and hadn't talked to her since she popped up at the crib on that rah-rah bullshit. I was over her and her temper tantrums. If it wasn't about Jay or the child she was carrying, she had no reason to hit my line. I would never turn my back on Jay, regardless of what his mother and I were going through. He was only a child, and lil' man was innocent. To him, I may as well have been his daddy, and no matter what happened, I would always honor that.

I made a quick store run, then stopped by Chick-fil-A to

grab Amor and me something to eat. For some reason, she loved that spot, but to me, it was overrated. I would have preferred a homecooked meal because my girl could throw down in the kitchen, but since she was tired, I didn't push the issue. Besides, I wanted to stay on her good side where I appeared to be for the moment.

When I got back to the house, Amor was on the couch, waiting for me. She had on one of my tank tops with a pair of those sexy ass boy shorts she loved to wear around the house. I wanted to taste her so bad my mouth started to water. Amor wasn't fucking with me on that level and would probably shut me down, but it was worth a try.

I set the food on the table in front of her and went in for a kiss. To my surprise, she didn't curse me out. Instead, she allowed me to kiss her. My hands palmed her breasts before making their way to her private area. I eased her boy shorts to the side and slid one of my fingers inside her. Amor's pussy was as wet as a river, and I couldn't wait to dive in head headfirst. The anticipation was killing me. I looked at her, silently asking for permission before I buried my head between her legs. Then I sucked on her clit like a baby sucking on a pacifier.

Amor moaned and grabbed the back of my head, pushing my tongue further into her pussy. I loved the way she grinded her pussy in my face. Moments later, her juices coated my throat and my beard.

"Can I feel you, baby?" I asked before stepping out of my joggers.

Amor didn't say a word, but she shook her head, and the look in her eyes said exactly what I wanted it to say.

I climbed on top of her and gently eased my dick inside. Her walls gripped and hugged my dick so tightly. I could tell she'd been missing me just as much as I missed her. As I made slow, passionate love to her, Amor wrapped her legs around me and started to fuck me from underneath. I was so excited that I found myself nutting quicker than I ever had before. I was a little embarrassed, but Amor seemed pleased, so I wasn't even tripping.

When we were done, Amor fell asleep peacefully in my arms as I held her. Something nagged at me to check my phone. I hadn't even looked at it since I got back to the house.

After the situation with Nina calling my phone, I started keeping it on do not disturb. I liked that shit because it still let me know who had called or texted me when I looked at my phone. All my niggas had been blowing my shit up for some reason. I already knew something bad had happened. Either something had gone wrong with a drug shipment, or someone was dead. I tried to mentally prepare myself for the worst before calling the last person who had called me, which was the homie Twan.

"What's good, my nigga? Everything straight?" I asked.

"Naw, nigga, everything ain't straight. Them niggas caught Derrick slipping, and he didn't pull through."

"Nigga, what? Run that to me again," I snapped, not wanting to believe what I'd just heard. There wasn't any fucking way my nigga was really gone.

"You heard me right. Derrick is gone, foo," Twan repeated, confirming my worst nightmare.

The news of Derrick's death hit a nigga like a ton of bricks. It was something I never saw coming. Of all people, some pussy ass niggas running up on him was unexpected. Derrick was the most laid back and chilled person in my whole crew. He didn't fuck with anyone and only got physical when he had to. For years, he'd been the peacemaker. Shit in the streets had been a lot less bloody because of him. See, I was a ticking time bomb, always ready to explode, while Derrick was the level-headed one who could always talk sense into me.

He was the only one I listened to, the only one I trusted with my operation and my life. Without him, shit would never move the same again. Guilt immediately kicked in, even though I knew death wasn't in my control. The truth was, bad shit happened, and sometimes people were just at the wrong place at the wrong time.

I blamed myself for not being around to help when he needed it. A nigga would have never tried him had I been around. I had so much drama going on in my personal life that I'd allowed it to get in the way of business. I guess we were all caught lacking. That was the main reason I tried to keep shit copasetic at home. With my chosen line of work, I couldn't have any distractions. The smallest distraction could cost me my life or someone else's life.

I dreaded having to face his mother and sisters. I knew they would instantly blame me for what happened. His mother begged him to cut dealings with the street life, and after he wouldn't budge, I assured her nothing would happen to him on my watch. Until then, I'd kept my promise because my word was all I had, and I stood on that.

By the time I hung up, Amor was awake and had heard my entire conversation with Twan. Her eyes watered, and I knew she was about to break down. Amor wasn't too fond of the niggas in my circle, but she loved herself some Derrick. They had a bond like no other. Even when she was mad at me, he could still get through to her and always smoothed things over between us. Derrick was the only nigga I trusted inside our home. I knew he would never try anything with Amor. She looked at him like one of her brothers or something. I introduced her to Derrick before she even met my family, so I knew she felt his death to the core, just like I did. Like the good woman she was, Amor tried to keep it together so she could be there for me.

"I know, baby. It's gon' be aight, though. I gotta hit the block for a minute and see what I can find out about who did this shit to Derrick," I informed her.

"No, baby, please don't go. What if them niggas still out there somewhere?" Amor fretted.

"Baby, I'm good. I'm not worried about no niggas fuckin' with me. You, of all people, should know that, Amor. Your food is right there on the table if you still want it. Try not to worry too much. I promise I'ma make it back home to you in one piece."

"Okay, keep me posted, Tay. Let me know if you find out anything, and please don't go getting yourself in any shit. Nothing you can do will bring Derrick back," she expressed.

"I know, baby, but I can't even promise you that. You know it's about to be war in these streets behind my boy."

My mind raced the whole way over to the block. When I pulled up, everyone was posted up outside. Even in an area filled with hard bodies, sadness lingered in the air. Everyone was fucked up behind what happened to Derrick. He was a real nigga, and we all fucked with him the long way. So far, no one had heard or seen anything, but with the way the streets talked, I was positive it wouldn't be long before someone got to running their mouth. Until then, all we could do was lay low and wait.

CHAPTER TEN
NINA

Not hearing from Dontavious had really started to fuck with my mental. He had even gone so far as to block my number, so I couldn't call his phone. When I tried to call him from Jay's phone, he blocked Jay's number too. I tried to call him a few times restricted in hopes that he would answer, but none of that shit worked. He was taking ignoring me to new lengths. Normally, all I had to do was throw some pussy in his face, and he would run back like nothing happened.

I knew Amor was back from her little trip and assumed that was the reason he was acting the way he was. I hated that bitch's existence and couldn't wait until the day she was out of the picture. She was ruining my fuckin' life, and it was because of her that Dontavious didn't want any dealings with me or our baby.

None of the shit was fair. I knew I was wrong for getting involved with him, knowing his heart was elsewhere, but he was just as wrong for approaching me, knowing he had a bitch at home. It wasn't my fault that I'd fallen for him, and it wasn't my fault that I wanted more. Dontavious needed to be held accountable for his actions, and I wasn't going to stop until I accomplished that mission. He couldn't continue to get away with all the shit he'd been doing. I knew eventually he'd get caught, but I didn't want to wait that long.

Karma wasn't coming fast enough for me, so I decided to take matters into my own hands and speed up that process. I thought about going back to the house and starting some shit but figured that wasn't the best idea. Instead, I sent Amor a request on Facebook, and once she accepted, I sent her a long, detailed message letting her know I was the one who called Tay's phone that morning and we'd been fooling around for three years. I left out the part about me being pregnant. That was some news I'd leave up to Dontavious to tell her.

I asked her if she was available to meet me for lunch, so I could answer any questions she had, and to my surprise, she agreed to meet me. Of course, I arranged for us to meet at a public location where there would be plenty of witnesses. So far, she'd been calm, but I knew she was feisty, and I wasn't trying to fight her crazy ass.

Less than two hours later, I pulled up to Killen's Steakhouse. Once I was seated, I nervously waited for Amor to get there. I'd seen her plenty of times in pictures, so I knew exactly who I was looking for. When she finally walked in, I waved at her. She walked over and sat directly across from me. The silence was so thick; we could have heard a pen drop. I was taken aback by Amor's beauty. Pictures didn't do her justice, and I immediately could see why Dontavious was so crazy about her.

I was interrupted from my thoughts by her clearing her throat. I guess she was wondering why the fuck I was staring at her so hard. Hell, at the time, I didn't know if I wanted her or her nigga. I would have taken both of them if she was into that kind of thing, but I could look at her and tell she wasn't the freaky type. On the other hand, I was down for anything, which was why he always ran to me to fulfill his sexual desires.

"Thanks for agreeing to meet me, Amor. As you know from our conversation on the phone, I'm Nina," I greeted.

"I'm aware of that, and according to you, Dontavious is your man. Correct?" Amor inquired.

"Yes, that's correct. Honestly, Dontavious and I have been dealing with each other for almost four years," I responded.

"Four years is a long ass time for a woman to be content with being a nigga's side piece," Amor sarcastically said.

"I could see how it would look that way to you, but it's way more to it than that. Our relationship is not just based on sex. We spend lots of time together, and he takes care of my son and me financially. Whatever we need from him, we get," I boasted.

"That's interesting, Nina. Do you want a cookie for that? I'm really not understanding why you invited me here. Is there anything else you need to shed some light on?" Amor interrogated.

"I just wanted to come to you woman to woman to let you know what's what because you know these niggas be lying and playing both sides. Dontavious loves me, and he's said he's going to leave you to be with me," I lied.

This bitch had the nerve to laugh out loud. "And let me guess, you actually believed him? No bitch can take my place unless I give it to her. That man you're so pressed about is my man, and he's going to be my man until the day I decide I don't want his trifling ass anymore," she snapped.

"I'm just letting you know, so you'll be prepared. Don't say I didn't try to give you a heads up."

"Look, bitch. I don't know what kind of games you're playing or what possessed you to roll out of bed and decide to fuck with me today. Clearly, Tay didn't tell you that I'm not the one to be fucked with, so since he didn't, I'm telling you to your face. Don't fuckin' play with me. Next time, I won't be so nice. Now, you have a great rest of the day. Oh, and lunch is on me," Amor responded as she threw a hundred-dollar bill on the table and got up to walk away.

I had to give it to her; she handled the shit better than I expected her to. I said so much off-the-wall shit to try to get under her skin, but nothing worked. Everything I threw at her, she ate and came back with something even harder. For the most part, Amor didn't even seem to be bothered by the fact that her nigga was cheating. It was like she had already accepted the fact that he wasn't hitting on shit. Maybe, it was time for me to join the club.

I'd wasted my time reaching out to Amor, but at least she knew who I was now. I was no longer a secret, and that was all I wanted in the first place. I knew it wouldn't be long before I heard from Dontavious. Amor didn't seem like the type who could keep shit to herself, and I was sure she was already cursing his ass out for playing on her top.

CHAPTER ELEVEN

TAY

"I wish you would learn how to keep your little hoes in line," Amor shouted from the other end of the phone.

If it wasn't one thing, it was another. We'd barely made up good, and now she was coming at me sideways about some more shit.

"What the hell are you talking about now, Amor? A nigga ain't even did shit. I'm trying to get the funeral arrangements together for my guy, and you want to call me with that nonsense," I responded.

I really didn't know what the fuck was wrong with her, but I had too much shit on my mind to care.

"I understand you're grieving, Tay, but you got me fucked up. You know that Nina bitch had the nerve to inbox me and tell me how y'all been fucking, and how you're there for her and her kid financially. She invited me to have lunch with her, and guess what? I took her up on her offer. This delusional bitch even had the nerve to tell me you plan on leaving me to be with her. Nigga, if that's the case, why the fuck haven't you left yet? I'm not in the business of keeping no nigga that don't wanna be kept," Amor ranted.

"That girl is lying, baby. I hope you didn't believe anything she had to say."

"Tay, that crazy ass girl ain't lying on you. Three years out of the six we've been together, you've been dealing with this delusional ass hoe. I see why she feels like you're her man."

"It's not like that, baby. Can we just talk about this when I get home?" I asked.

"Nigga, by the time you get here, I'll be gone. That bitch can have your pathetic ass!" Amor yelled and ended the call.

I was at a loss for words. I knew Nina would eventually do some crazy shit, but I wasn't expecting it to happen so soon. She was one bold bitch to not only inbox Amor but to invite her out for lunch, so they could discuss me. That was a new level of crazy for her. I was even more surprised that Amor decided to go. I was waiting for her to say she whooped her ass, but she never did.

The pregnancy never came up, so I knew I was in the clear on that part. I wondered why Nina left that out when she'd clearly told her everything else. That bitch was up to something, and I had to find out what it was. I wasn't the type of man who would put my hands on a woman, but Nina had me so mad I wanted to fold her ass up in a corner somewhere. She was playing a very dangerous game, one that she wasn't going to win. It made no sense for her to do all the shit she was doing, all because I didn't want to be with her. Apparently, it bothered her that I could let her go so easily, but I always told her ass she was replaceable.

Now was the wrong time for her to be coming at me sideways. I had too much on my plate, and I really wasn't in my right mind. Losing Derrick had taken a toll on me mentally and physically. Most days, I didn't know if I was coming or fuckin' going. I tried to calm down before going to check Nina about her disrespect once again, but at that moment, nothing in the world could have calmed me down. I was beyond pissed the fuck off. Nina was really out to fuck up everything I'd worked so hard for. I could feel my whole world crumbling at my feet. I couldn't really be mad at her, though, because I was the one responsible for everything I was going through.

As a man in a relationship, I never should have approached Nina. I was always honest with her from the very beginning, but this was one situation that honesty didn't matter in. I regretted keeping it so real with the bitch and wished I'd just told her whatever I thought she wanted to hear like I'd done with the others. I should've fucked her ass and got the fuck on instead of making her feel special. That shit went right to her big ass head. I grabbed my phone, went to the settings so I could unblock her, and called her a few times.

This bitch had the nerve to not answer any of my calls, which pissed me off even more. I didn't want to just pop up at her house in the condition I was in. I respected Jay too much to do all that arguing and shit in front of him. But Nina left me no choice. I couldn't just let the shit slide, and I wouldn't be satisfied until I told her ass off. She thought she was doing something by ignoring me, but I guess she'd forgotten I had a key to the house. When I walked in, she was in the kitchen, fixing herself a glass of wine.

"Bitch, what the fuck are you doing? How the hell you claim you pregnant and you drinking and shit? Are you even pregnant foreal, or are you just trying to keep up some shit?" I interrogated.

"Nigga, please. One glass of wine is not going to hurt anything. Besides, it's safe to drink red wine. If you don't believe me, you can google it and see for yourself," Nina claimed.

"It doesn't even matter right now. I wouldn't give a fuck if you were drinking bleach."

"So, fuck me and your baby, huh?" Nina questioned.

"Bitch, you said it, not me. Why the fuck did you contact Amor? What are you trying to do, Nina?" I asked, trying my hardest not to let my anger get the best of me.

"I just thought she deserved to know what was going on with us, Dontavious. You weren't man enough to tell her, so I did it for you. Now, we can finally be together."

"Nina, are you fuckin' serious? Didn't I tell you that even if I wasn't with Amor, I wouldn't be with your delusional ass? You're even crazier than I thought you were."

"Is that any way to talk to the mother of your child, Dontavious? I think you should have a little more respect for me than you do."

"This is my last time telling you to stay the fuck away from Amor. Leave us the fuck alone. I don't want anything else to do with you, and as far as the baby goes, I'll see you in court."

"Nigga, you better be glad I didn't tell that bitch how you nutted all in this good pussy. Then you would really be in the doghouse. But I figured I'd let you tell her the good news."

"So, you really think this shit is funny, huh, Nina?"

"It's all fun and games until Nina has the gun, baby. I told you I would have the last laugh, didn't I?"

Nina left me standing in the kitchen looking crazy and walked upstairs to the bedroom. I wasn't done with the conversation, so I waited for her to come back downstairs. After she didn't return, I followed her to the room. This crazy bitch was standing in the middle of the floor with a black lingerie set on. She had the nerve to give me that seductive look as if I even wanted to touch her ass. I was disgusted by her.

"Nina, put some clothes on. I don't know what you think is about to happen, but it's not."

"Dontavious, I want some dick, and you're not leaving here until you give it to me."

"You done lost your damn mind foreal, Nina. I gotta go."

"Nigga, you're not going no fuckin' where. Obviously, you didn't get the memo that I'm calling the shots now."

"You right about that. I didn't get that memo. I think you should step away from the wine for a little while."

As I was about to walk back down the stairs, Nina stood in front of me, so I couldn't leave. I tried to move her, and she yanked back, which resulted in her losing her balance, and she fell down the stairs.

"Nina, what the fuck did you just do, man? Damn!" I knew not to touch her or move her, but I could hear her breathing, so that was a good thing.

I called 911 and reported the accident. Since I had nothing to hide and I had done nothing wrong, I even waited for the police and paramedics to arrive. I hadn't so much as laid a finger on her, so I wasn't worried about a damn thing.

I was told to come down to the station for additional questioning, but once I got there, it turned into some other shit. Come to find out, Nina told them I pushed her down the stairs and that I'd come over with the intent to cause harm to her and her unborn baby. She'd given them this whole story, and if I didn't know better, even I would have believed it. I ended up getting booked and processed for domestic violence.

When I finally got my one call, I called Amor to let her know what happened and to tell her to contact my lawyer. Amor was pissed, and I knew that was the end for us. The only thing she ever asked of me was to not embarrass her or have her out there looking like a fool, and I'd managed to do both of those things. There was nothing I could do or say to make things right between us. All the money and shopping sprees in the world couldn't fix it. I'd really fucked up, and I had to eat that shit.

My mind drifted off to Nina and the way she fell down the stairs. I wondered if she was okay. I'd never witnessed anything like that up close and personal, and it was an image I would never forget. With Nina acting the way she was, I started to believe she did the shit on purpose. I wondered if the baby was okay too. I'd watched a lot of movies, and when something like that occurred, the baby usually didn't make it. I didn't want to be the father of Nina's baby, but I didn't want the baby to die, either. All the shit was crazy, and I really couldn't make sense of it.

I knew Nina was that way because of me and my actions. I could have handled shit with her so differently, but I never expected things to get so far out of control. Getting some pussy on the side wasn't even worth all the trouble it caused me. As a result of my careless ways, I was about to lose the best thing that ever happened to me. The money and shit were cool, but it didn't mean shit without having someone to share it with. All I could do was pray that Amor would find it in her heart to forgive me. It wouldn't happen overnight, and I didn't expect it to. I just needed it to happen.

I hoped my lawyer could get me out of the mess I was in. With all the money I was paying his ass, he'd better be on his shit. I couldn't believe Nina lied and said I put my hands on her. I'd never put my hands on a woman before unless it was while we were in the act of fucking. She was really taking things too far. With the way shit got around, I knew my family would hear about it soon. I already knew my momma would be so disappointed in me. She damn sure wasn't gon' like the fact that I'd gotten someone pregnant other than her beloved Amor.' I dreaded having that conversation with her. I hated when she was disappointed in me, but there was nothing I could do to change everything that had happened.

On top of everything else, Derrick's funeral was in two days, and I wasn't trying to miss it. I wouldn't have been able to live with myself if I did. Everything was so fucked up, and I honestly couldn't see a way out. For the first time, I was in a dark place and didn't know what the outcome would be.

CHAPTER TWELVE
AMOR

The phone call I'd just gotten was one I never expected to receive. I could only imagine how Tay felt about having to use his one call to call and tell me the shit he had to. The conversation left me completely speechless. All I could do was listen to him as he chopped my feelings down more and more with every word he said. Hearing him tell me another bitch was pregnant and that the baby was most likely his tore my heart into little pieces. I didn't want to believe it, but I had no choice since I was hearing it straight from the horse's mouth.

I knew Tay like the back of my hand, and I didn't believe for a second that he'd pushed Nina down the stairs. Tay was a lot of things, but he had never been abusive. In the years we'd been together, the most he'd ever done was pushed me. I had the kind of mouth that would make a nigga want to hem my little ass up, so that was to be expected. Nina was trying to set Tay up, and although I was mad at him, I refused to let that shit happen.

It was crazy how Tay didn't even realize he was fucking

with someone who wasn't mentally stable. From the day I met Nina, I could see that she wasn't all there in the head. Or, as the old people used to say, her elevator didn't go all the way to the top. The bitch was beyond delusional. I could tell she believed everything she told me, and that was scary. She'd made up all those lies in her head and couldn't make sense of them not being factual. Maybe she did love Tay. Who was I to say? I wasn't in the mix when they did whatever they did in their weird ass relationship, but for him to invest three years into her, it had to be something that kept him holding on.

Nina was beautiful, and she had a body on her. I could see why he was attracted to her, but that still was no excuse for him to play with her feelings or her emotions. Men didn't understand how dangerous toying with a woman's heart could be, and that was why he was sitting his ass in the county jail.

After placing a call to Tay's lawyer and bringing him up to speed with what he was dealing with, I made a few more calls to find out where Nina was located. Luckily, she ended up being at St. David's Medical Center, and I happened to have a friend who worked there. She worked in admissions, so I would have no problem getting in to see Nina. I had to find a way to get her to drop the charges. Either that, or I needed to get her to admit that Tay didn't push her. I had my recorder on me, and getting her confession on tape was all I needed for them to release Tay.

I knew I was probably making a mistake by going to see her, and I was probably the last person she wanted to see, but I had to do what I had to do. Regardless of what Tay had done, I couldn't just leave him hanging, especially when I knew he was innocent. It was crazy the things that love could make a woman do. I felt like I was in a Lifetime movie or something. Tay's dick wasn't even good enough to have her carrying on like she was doing. Maybe he was hitting her with some different positions or something. Whatever the case, it wasn't that damn deep. There was much better dick out there; I knew that for sure. When I made it to the front desk, I was happy to see that Brittany was indeed working.

"Hey, Amor! Long time no see. What are you doing here, girl?"

"I need to see Nina O'Bryant," I stated.

"Are you a relative or—"

"Brittany, cut the bullshit," I said, cutting her off. "I know you've heard everything that happened. Tay didn't push that girl, and I just need to get her to say it, so I can get him out of jail. That bitch is bat shit crazy."

"Yeah, I'm aware. I'm going to let you back there, but please try to keep the commotion to a minimum. I could lose my job behind doing this," she said.

"I know you could, girl. I promise to be on good behavior. I wouldn't put you in a position to lose your job," I promised.

"Okay, girl. You have fifteen minutes. My shift will be over, and my replacement will be coming in."

"Thanks, I won't even take that long. Good looking out, B."

I took a deep breath before I knocked on the door and entered the hospital room. Nina's eyes got big as hell when she realized it was me. They looked like deer eyes when they were caught in headlights. *Yeah, bitch it's me,* I said to myself. I knew I had to tell her whatever she wanted to hear, and I was prepared to say the dumbest shit because I knew she would eat it up.

"What are you doing here?" Nina asked.

"I come in peace, Nina. I'm not on any bullshit. I wanted to see if you were okay. I heard what happened," I responded.

"Well, I have a few fractured bones, but I didn't lose my baby. I know that's what you wanted," Nina taunted.

"I don't know what kind of monster you think I am, Nina,

but I would never wish any harm on you or your unborn. I'm glad to hear that you both are doing fine," I insisted.

"Yeah, I bet you are. Okay, you can leave now. I'm trying to get some rest."

"I just have one more question, and I will gladly get out of your hair."

"What is it? What could you possibly have to ask me?"

"The police report says that you told them Tay pushed you. I just don't believe that. Tay would never do something like that. Why did you tell them that? I mean, am I wrong? Did that bastard really do that to you?" I quizzed.

"Dontavious did not push me. He would never put his hands on me. He loves me too much to hurt me or our baby. I was just mad at him. I was so mad at him for still choosing you. He always chooses you," Nina admitted.

"I figured that was the case. Well, Tay is in jail, and unless you drop those charges on him, he will probably be there for a while. I don't know what is going on between the two of you, but you can consider me out of the picture. I packed my shit, and I am no longer in the house with him. You wanted my spot so bad, Nina, so I'm giving it to you," I responded before I walked out of the room.

Once I was back in my car, I forwarded the message to Tay's lawyer and powered my phone off. I was sure he could handle the rest from there. Hell, I'd done his job for him, and I didn't even know why the fuck I cared so much. At that moment, all I wanted was to be with Chosen and to feel his big strong arms wrapped around me. I couldn't believe I'd missed out on a chance to be with him, only to find out that Tay had a whole side bitch with a baby on the way.

Nina was a different kind of special. I'd never met a bitch who was happier to be some cole slaw. I headed to the house and started to pack up as much of my belongings as I could. I didn't plan to be in the house when Tay got there. It was time for him to pay for the actions he chose to take.

I could no longer turn the cheek and pretend that I wasn't hurting. I had wasted so much time waiting for him to change, and I didn't have any more time to waste on him. It was clear that he had no intention of changing. He was perfectly content with being exactly who he was, and that no longer worked for me. I knew better, and I wanted better out of a partner. I wished Tay nothing but the best.

Nina had fallen down a flight of stairs and still managed to be pregnant, so I took that as it was meant for her to have Tay's baby. He'd been with her for all those years, so now he was free to do so without having to hide it. I still couldn't bring myself to contact Chosen, though. I feared being rejected or hearing that he no longer felt the same about me.

CHAPTER THIRTEEN

NINA

I beamed on the inside after hearing Amor say that she was done with Dontavious. Her words sounded like a sweet melody to my ears. I'd been waiting for that moment for an eternity, but I was glad she finally came to her senses. All it took was me getting pregnant to put some fire under her ass. Now that the time had finally arrived, I didn't even know what to make of it.

Dontavious made it clear he wanted absolutely nothing to do with me. He referred to me as crazy and delusional, and he basically said I needed to get a grip on reality. That was just like a man to make a woman crazy and then turn around and blame her for being crazy. Hearing him say those harsh things hurt me more than anything. I was left trying to find a way to make things right with him. Having him locked up was taking shit too far, especially since I'd done so under false pretenses. That wasn't going to help my case—if anything, it sealed my fate. Some shit, there was no coming back from, and I knew that all too well.

I shouldn't have done it in the first place, but Dontavious

made me so fuckin' mad. He didn't care about shit. Not my feelings, not the baby, not the fact that my heart was literally crying out for him. Amor was the only person that nigga cared about. Hell, maybe I should have pushed her ass down the stairs instead. Her being completely out of the picture was the only way we would ever have a fair chance at happiness. Leaving him was a good start, though, and I appreciated her for getting the fuck out of my way.

I was in so much pain after the accident at the house, and I just knew I'd miscarried our baby. I couldn't believe it when the doctor came in to examine me, and my baby's heartbeat was still strong and as healthy as ever. He or she was going to be a tough little cookie. Until that very moment, I never really cared, nor did I feel any kind of bond with the child I was carrying. It wasn't like I wanted another child anyway or that I'd gotten pregnant on purpose. Obviously, things happened for a reason, and it was meant for me to be a mother again.

The thought of going through everything alone again like I was doing with Jay scared the shit out of me. But as their mother, I would do anything but fold. One thing about a mother—for the little humans we birthed, we would always make a way. I would make sure both of my kids were loved and taken care of whether a nigga chose to be around or not.

Dontavious wasn't a bad person, and I knew he would eventually have a change of heart. One day he would understand that I was coming from a place of love and that everything I did was for us. Maybe I went about things the wrong way, and I could admit that. I called the police department to ask that the charges be dropped and was told that Dontavious had already made bail. I wondered how the fuck he was able to pull that shit off. But then I remembered he knew people in very high places, and there wasn't any telling who he had on his payroll.

Dontavious was smart, and he always had a plan in motion. That was how he managed to get out of all the shit he got into on the streets. That nigga had so many bodies on him, but he'd never served time for anything a day in his life. I was happy to know he was out. Now, I had to get better, so I could get the hell out of the hospital and get my man back. It wasn't going to be easy, but it had to be done.

————

Two days went by, and I still hadn't heard a word from Dontavious. He had every right to be mad at me, but he could have at least called or come by to check on our baby and me. The more time that passed, the more I started to realize that I didn't mean shit to him. Even with Amor supposedly out of the picture, he treated me like a nobody. A mixture of different emotions consumed me. I was mad, sad, disappointed, and downright embarrassed. There was no way in hell I was out there making a complete fool out of myself over a man who didn't care enough about me to pick up the phone and call me.

Life was crazy, but then again, karma came in many forms. Maybe that was my payback for dealing with Tay, knowing he had a woman at home. Karma was an even bigger bitch than I was.

CHAPTER FOURTEEN

TAY

I was released from jail just in time to go home and get prepared for Derrick's funeral, which was taking place in a few hours. Once again, Amor had come through for me. Despite all the shit I put her through, she still chose to be in my corner. Had it not been for her recording Nina's confession, my black ass would have still been in jail. The system didn't play that domestic violence bullshit. I couldn't imagine what it took out of her to visit Nina in the hospital. That's why she would always be a realer woman than most.

I wasn't at all surprised when I got home and discovered that Amor was gone. Most of her clothes and stuff were gone too. I couldn't even trip because I had that shit coming and then some. When she told me she was leaving, I thought she was just talking shit as she always did. I figured she wanted to get a reaction out of me. But her really being gone was something I wasn't prepared for. I wanted to believe she would be back once she had a little time to calm down, but everything about that shit let me know it was permanent. I guess the saying was true, every dog had their day, and that day was mine.

I couldn't just sit around and sulk in self-pity; I had to pull myself together. After I hopped in the shower, I walked over to my closet in search of the perfect suit to wear. Once I was dressed, I headed to the spot to pick some of the fellas up so we could pay our respects to our brother together. The shit was still so unreal, but the closer we got to the church where his service was being held, the more reality kicked in. We were really about to see Derrick for the last time. I hated funerals and didn't even attend my own family members' funerals. In this case, I had to make an exception because that nigga was closer to me than family.

When we walked in, his mother walked up to me and hugged me tightly. She thanked me for paying for his burial arrangements and told me not to be so hard on myself. She wanted me to know they didn't blame me for what happened to Derrick. That shit lifted a weight from my shoulders, and I felt ten times lighter. I didn't believe her because a part of me did feel like I was responsible. I wasn't going to rest until I made whoever was responsible for Derrick's death pay. It was his funeral today, but it would be someone else's soon.

I was shocked when I saw Amor crying her eyes out. Something told me to keep walking and not bother her, but I wanted to be there for her like she had always been for me. I took a seat on the pew beside her, and she instantly buried her head in my shoulder. I didn't even care that her makeup was ruining the expensive ass suit I wore. I comforted her and told her everything was going to be okay. When the funeral was over, Amor said she wasn't able to go to the repast or to hang with the family afterward. I assumed she just didn't want to be around me, and that was okay too.

The rest of my day was spent with Derrick's family. I couldn't just turn my back on them. Now that he was gone, I had to make sure they were straight. Derrick didn't play about his mama or his sisters. Therefore, I couldn't play about them either.

Once I was finally home and alone with my thoughts, I had some time to reflect. I needed to own up to all the shit I did. I owed both Amor and Nina apologies. Though I didn't do it purposely, maybe in a way, I did lead Nina on. And when it came to Amor, I was dead ass wrong for the way I misused her when all she did was love me from day one. Not being a good man to her would always be one of my biggest regrets, and losing her would remain my biggest L. Niggas fumbled good women every day, but Amor didn't deserve any of what I put her through.

I called Nina and apologized to her for my actions. I let her know that I didn't want to be in a relationship with her, but we could still be cool. I still wanted to be there for her and Jay, and once the baby was born and I found out if it was mine or not, I wanted to be there for my child as well. Nina needed to know that she wasn't the problem. There was nothing wrong with her; I just wasn't in any position to give her what she wanted from me. She would've been the perfect woman for another man, but at the time, that man just wasn't me.

My apology to Amor would have to wait. She needed space to heal and find herself again. I respected that, and hell, if nothing else, I owed her that. No matter what happened between us, I would continue to hold her down and be there for her. Amor never had to work a day in her life if she chose not to. I was forever indebted to her, and I was going to make she was straight no matter what terms we were on.

If there was a chance that we could reconcile, I was with it, but if she was really done with my ass, I had to accept that too. I damn sure wasn't going to stop trying, though. I couldn't just completely give up on her because I loved her way too much to do that. Only time would tell what would happen between us.

CHAPTER FIFTEEN

AMOR

SIX WEEKS LATER

Tay's family reunion was the last place I wanted to go, especially with everything we were going through. Yet, there I was, forcing myself to get dressed so I could accompany him. It was hard for me to fake the funk, so I knew I would fail miserably when it came to pretending like Tay and I were the perfect couple. His family always assumed we were so happy, but if only they knew the half. I wasn't the type to involve people in my business, so I would never speak badly about him to his family. I had a very close relationship with them. They loved me, and I loved them to death as well.

We'd known about the gathering for the longest, and even though we weren't on good terms, Tay had managed to talk me into tagging along with him anyway. Showing up without me would raise all kinds of red flags. Tay wasn't up for explaining anything to them, and I could somewhat understand that.

After finding out about Tay possibly having a baby by that crazy bitch Nina, I lost the little respect I had for him. I couldn't even stand to be under the same roof. I hated his ass with a passion for allowing me to be embarrassed. I couldn't stand for a bitch to have one up on me, and Nina had exactly that. As bad as I wanted to whoop her ass, I couldn't even be mad at her. She had all the receipts I needed to confirm that my nigga wasn't shit. It wasn't like I didn't know that shit anyway, but damn! Tay was known for fucking off, but what he had with Nina was something deeper. He was supporting the bitch and her child financially.

On top of that, he had the nerve to be careless enough to run up in her raw. Now, he was trying to say the baby wasn't his, but I wasn't boo-boo the fool. I didn't know Nina, nor did I know anything about her, but she didn't strike me as a liar. It was clear she wanted what I had, but almost everything that rolled off her tongue was believable.

There was only one thing she claimed that I knew was a lie. She swore up and down that Tay told her he would leave me for her, and I called bullshit. Not on any cocky shit, but there wasn't a bitch walking God's green earth who could make that man leave me. Yeah, he may have done his share of dirt, but that nigga worshiped the ground I walked on. These bitches would have been better off waiting for me to leave his ass because waiting for him to walk away from me, they would've been waiting forever.

Three years... I still couldn't wrap my mind around the fact that Tay had been fucking with the rachet ass bitch for three years. I wondered what made the bitch want to suddenly speak up when she'd been quiet for so long. That only meant one thing; she wasn't getting what she wanted out of the deal. Nina had these high expectations that she could change him and mold him into the man she wanted him to be. That shit was relatable because I think all women believed that stupid shit a time or two. That was still me, and it was exactly the reason I found myself still holding on, years later.

I felt like a damn fool when I could have been off with Chosen, living my best damn life. With him, I wouldn't have to put up with the disrespect and emotional abuse I was dealing with. Every fiber of my being wanted to reach out to Chosen, but I didn't because I had been blowing him off ever since I got back home.

I liked Chosen and didn't want to lead him on or make him feel like I was playing with his feelings if things didn't work out the way he expected them to. I was confused and needed time to properly heal before jumping headfirst into another relationship anyway. Chosen was so sure he had everything figured out and wanted what he wanted without considering what I wanted or needed. I would always have a soft spot for him, and he'd always be known as the man I let get away. Some days, I couldn't get him off my mind. He was like a drug or something, and I was somewhat addicted. It was hard to watch him call my phone or read his texts and not be able to respond. I was doing what was best for us both, or at least that's what I told myself.

Things between Tay and I were going so damn good. It was like he'd done a complete 180 overnight. He was spending more time in the house, catering to my wants as well as my needs, and we hadn't had a single argument or disagreement since I'd been back from my trip until the shit popped up with Nina and her unborn. The more time I had to process it, the more I started to not give a fuck. Her being pregnant didn't have a damn thing to do with me. Hell, I didn't have to rock a baby or change any pampers, and I damn sure wasn't going to lose any sleep. I was still free to come and go as I pleased without having a little person attached to me.

That shit really wasn't as big of a flex as she tried to make it out to be. Even a baby wasn't enough to make Tay change his selfish ass ways, and a part of me felt sorry for her because she thought that having his kid would be the solution to their problems. Nothing could change a man except him wanting to change.

Of course, Tay going out and getting another bitch pregnant hurt me. That shit cut me like a knife, actually, but I couldn't let the hurt consume me. What I allowed would only continue. I tried not to even think about it. I wanted to believe the baby wasn't his, but even that didn't change the fact that it was a possibility.

I had packed all my shit and had been staying with Leilani ever since. Going to my parent's house was out of the question because I didn't want them that deep in my business. I was in the bathroom getting dressed when Leilani walked in with her nose turned up. I already knew she was about to talk her shit. I shook my head and braced myself for what she was about to say.

"I can't believe you're really about to go to this family reunion with him after all the shit he did to you. Shit, I don't get it. Why the hell he can't take his maybe babymama with him?"

"Leilani, please don't start. I've known about this function for a long time now. Besides, I promised him I would go. I can't just change my mind at the last minute. You know I love his mama, and I don't want to disappoint her or hurt her feelings," I expressed.

"Girl, please. Niggas' mamas be the fakest. She probably already knows about all the foul shit he's been on. Don't be surprised if she's playing both sides just like Tay's ass is."

"She's not like that. His mama doesn't play that bullshit at all. I know for a fact she's oblivious to what's been going on, just like I was," I responded.

"I don't know, Amor. I just hate the way that nigga played in your face. I'm glad you left the house, but you need to leave his ass alone for good. I know you're not waiting to find out if that damn baby is his or not before you make a decision, are you?"

Leilani finally asked the question I'd been dreading.

"No, I'm not waiting for that per se, but I do want to know if the baby is his," I admitted.

"Girl, fuck all that. You're better than me to be dealing with all this shit you don't even have to be dealing with. That nigga made his bed, so let his ass lie there. He didn't care about your damn feelings when he was out fucking random bitches unprotected," Leilani pointed out, and I knew she was right.

"I know, Leilani. You don't have to keep throwing the shit in my face. I get it."

"Anyway, have you talked to Chosen? I haven't heard you mention him at all lately."

"No, I haven't talked to him. Before this baby incident popped up, Tay and I decided to work on our relationship. I didn't need the distraction, but I think he's supposed to be in town for something going on with his family."

"I think you should hit him up and set up something so you can see him. Hopefully, he can talk some sense into you."

"Girl, Chosen probably doesn't have his mind on me. He's probably moved on to the next pretty face by now. I don't want to just hit him up out of the blue like that," I told her.

"I'm with you on whatever you decide because you're my girl, but I think you're making a huge mistake."

"I think I am, too, Leilani," I responded as I shrugged and continued to apply my makeup.

"I'll see you when you get back, friend. Elijah is taking me out for lunch and a movie."

"Aww, that's sweet. Have fun."

"I will, girl. Try to enjoy yourself at the reunion, too," Leilani sarcastically said.

A few minutes later, Tay pulled up outside and blew the horn. I looked in the mirror one more time and was satisfied with what I saw. The outfit I had on hugged my curves perfectly. I still looked good, but I was also dressed appropriately to be around Tay's family members. I already knew that when we got there, his mama would make me put on one of those ugly ass t-shirts they had ordered anyway. I wasn't tripping, though, because I would do anything for that lady. I hated that things were about to end with Tay and me because I'd gotten so attached to his family. That was one of the hardest parts of letting go and starting over.

"Hey, Tay," I dryly greeted as I got in the car and shut the door.

"Hey, baby, you look so good. I miss you so much. Thank you for agreeing to go to the family reunion with me. This was something you didn't even have to do."

"I know it wasn't something I had to do, but it's fine. Let's just go and get it over with. I can't be there all day because I have something else to do later," I let him know.

"Can I ask what you have planned for later?" Tay quizzed.

"No, you can't. What I do no longer concerns you, Tay. You see I'm not questioning you about a damn thing."

"Oh, okay, I see what it is. Bet. I gotcha. Just know I better not catch you," he threatened.

"Catch me doing what? I'm not lying, and I damn sure don't have anything to hide. Single people do what they want."

When we pulled up to the park where everything was taking place, I tried to get myself in character for the act I was about to put on. Putting a smile on my face was nearly impossible, but I did the shit anyway. Tay knew I didn't feel comfortable, and he knew I wasn't up to lying to his people, especially not his mother. I hoped and prayed she didn't ask any awkward questions because, knowing me, I would cave and let her in on everything. Hell, she needed to know she had a grandchild on the way. She'd been nagging us to give her a grandchild for the longest, and ironically, another bitch was about to give her one.

The park was packed, and there were a lot of family members I had yet to meet. Tay paraded me around like I was a trophy or something. He bragged to everyone about how good a woman I was and even lied and said he'd be popping the question any day now. I rolled my eyes at his bullshit antics to let him know I didn't appreciate the games he was playing.

I spent most of my time around the little children. A little girl who couldn't have been any more than three years old followed me around the entire time. It was crazy how little kids flocked to me and how I was so good with them but never wanted any of my own. It made me wonder why I was still holding on because I for damn sure wasn't about to play that stepmother role. Had the details surrounding the situation been different, I may have felt differently, but it was what it was.

I'd purposely kept my distance from Tay's mom and sisters since we got there, but his mother found her way over to me.

"Hey, my sweet girl. How are you doing?" she greeted.

"Hey, Mama. How are you?" I asked as she pulled me in for a hug.

"I'm fine. I didn't expect to see you here," she said, getting straight to the point.

"Why wouldn't I be here?"

"I heard about that mess of a situation that son of my mine has got himself into, Amor. A hard head makes a soft ass, and I told him that a long time ago. I hate to say it, but Tay is just like that trifling ass daddy of his," she continued.

"Oh, so you know you're about to be a grandmother?" I asked.

I was relieved that everything was out in the open, and I no longer had to bite my tongue. That shit hurt to do.

"Word travels quick, Amor. That's my son, and I love him to death, but I'm telling you this because I'm a woman, and I have been where you are right now. Leave his ass. Don't stick around and be miserable. Go be happy, Amor. You deserve to be. Tay messed up, and ain't no way he can fix it this time," she verbalized.

"It's so hard, Ma. One day I feel like I'm ready to walk away, and the next, I don't want to. I don't know what to do. I love your son, and I know he loves me. But he hurt me to the core, and I don't think I'll ever be able to forgive him. How can I accept him having a child by another woman and a childish female like Nina anyway?" I asked.

"It can be done, but it's going to take hard work from both of you. That's if you want to stick around and fight for your relationship. If you know in your heart it's over, then let it go. He doesn't know I know this, but when he does come to me and is ready to talk about it, you already know I'm going to let his black behind have it."

"Yes, ma'am, I know you are. Thanks for the talk. I needed that more than you know," I expressed.

"I love you, Amor, and I'm sorry my son doesn't realize what he has in front of him," she said.

"I love you too, Mama. Yeah, I'm sorry he doesn't either," I responded just as Tay walked up to us.

"What are my two favorite women over here yapping about?" Tay asked.

"Nothing, we're just catching up on some things," I told him.

"Come on, baby. I want you to meet some of my cousins." Tay grabbed me by the hand.

I couldn't believe what the fuck I saw. I looked around for Ashton Kutcher to pop out and let me know I was being Punk'd. There was no way in the hell Chosen was standing right in front of me. My heartbeat sped up and then slowed down again. I wanted to jump on him, hug him tight, and wrap my arms around his neck. But I had to play the shit cool. I knew it was a small ass world, but what were the odds of Tay and Chosen being related and cousins at that?

"Baby, this is my cousin Chosen. Chosen, this is my girl, Amor," Tay introduced us.

To be continued....

AFTERWORD

I hope you enjoyed this book. Please leave an honest review. Whether it's good or bad, I look forward to your feedback. I appreciate your support. Thanks for reading.

LET'S GET CONNECTED!

Facebook: Tosha Lavette
Instagram: Tosh_lavette
TikTok: tosha_lavette
Facebook Reading Group: Book Ish&Chill
Twitter @Authoress-Vette

ALSO BY TOSHA LAVETTE

Made in United States
Orlando, FL
03 March 2023

30639401R00086